Praise for *The Unraveling Thread*

"Priscilla Cogan reveals a modern family's discovery of a multifaceted genetic disorder *(Velo-Cardio-Facial Syndrome)* amidst the daily challenges of their busy lives. The story of Sola WcWhinnie is about the love of her divergent family and the road to understanding her biological roots. *The Unraveling Thread* is a poignant realization of the consequences of genetic disorders, the limits of medical science, the power of knowledge, the courage of parents, and the resilience of the human mind."

—William D. Graf, M.D.,
Child Neurologist

"As a reader I loved the clever plot; as a writer I reveled in the music of the words (walk in soft moccasins. I know where I put feet.); as a Christian, I could identify with each character's battle for faith—in themselves and in something beyond themselves. Best of all, Priscilla Cogan wraps the story around life's most important truth: it's all about love."

—Sue Harrison,
author of *Mother Earth Father Sky*

"I read with great pleasure *The Unraveling Thread*. Once started I had trouble putting it down and even now I wonder what is happening in the McWinnie household. I want to hear more of Agatha's story. This book crackles with the familiar challenges of women's lives; their complexity and poignancy. Powerful word images evoke characters replete with humor, courage and affection. And Agatha carries the transforming archetype of the wise woman, the mature Persephone, that is so desperately needed by women today."

—Jennifer Barker,
author of *The Goddess Within*

"*The Unraveling Thread* is the heartwarming story of independent, loveable, and generous characters whose individual threads weave a rich family tapestry. Written almost totally in dialogue, the story reads like the script for an HBO series. In her many novels, Priscilla Cogan has expertly woven Native American beliefs into modern western culture with understanding and compassion, a job for which she is justly qualified—Ph.D. clinical psychologist and pipe carrier—someone who knows fully the way of the pipe."

—Evelyn Wolfson,
author of *From the Earth to Beyond the Sky*

THE
UNRAVELING
THREAD

A NOVEL BY

PRISCILLA COGAN

TWO CANOES PRESS
Hopkinton, Massachusetts

Two Canoes Press
PO Box 334
Hopkinton, MA 01748
www.TwoCanoesPress.com

Jacket and book design by Arrow Graphics, Inc.
Watertown, Massachusetts
info@arrow1.com

Jacket illustration by Victoria Krassa
Author's photograph by Duncan Sings-Alone

Manufactured in the United States of America

Publisher's Cataloging-in-Publication
(Provided by Quality Books, Inc.)

Cogan, Priscilla, 1947-
    The unraveling thread / by Priscilla Cogan.
    p. cm.
    ISBN-13: 978-1-929590-11-7
    ISBN-10: 1-929590-11-3

    1. Indians of North America—Fiction. 2. Domestic
fiction. 3. Psychological fiction.   I. Title.

PS3553.O4152U57 2008   813'.54
                                  QBI08-600053

ACKNOWLEDGMENTS

It's dangerous being a family member, friend, or acquaintance of a novelist. We are thieves by nature—pilfering bits and pieces of stories, names, odd but interesting habits, bad jokes, and personal observations. It's a cut and paste job, creating collages within the structures and strictures of plot, character, landscape, and colored by the fiery underground of the novelist's psyche.

I want to acknowledge those people who might recognize a piece of themselves or their imaginations in the pages of *The Unraveling Thread*:

Christy Parson, my niece, who has taught me about what it's like to live with VCFS, the ability to endure great physical challenges, while maintaining both a sensitivity to other people and a belief in the goodness of humanity.

Polly Parson, my sister, a veritable saint, who is a source of information and comfort to countless VCFS parents and unflagging support to me. Dr. William Parson, my brother-in-law, who educated me about errant DNA while working on the biochemistry of VCFS.

Mary Cheadle Babl of Hummingbird Editing who kept me cogent in my grammatical wanderings. Alvert Badalian of Arrow Graphics Inc. for the design elements of the book production.

Wendy Williams, the late Dr. Frances Cogan, Barbara McBride-Smith, Dr. Nancielee Holbrook, Nancy Kotting, David Kaczynski, F. Earle Beaton, Christina Duncan Johnson, the Young family who introduced me to Duxbury, Mass, Scalawag our crazy Sheltie, and Masterpeace Dog Training Facility who tried their very best to tame him.

Last, but not least by any stretch of the imagination, is Duncan Sings-Alone: husband, best friend, colleague, and muse—from whom I always steal my best lines.

For Christy Parson

The web of our life is of a mingled yarn,
good and ill together...

—William Shakespeare

PROLOGUE

"I want to tell you this story, before I lose the thread of it," exclaimed Opal, smoothing down a flyaway strand of her white hair. "Once you let it slip, the thread will disappear into a maze of competing realities. Hold onto it tightly, dear ones. It's all that stands between you and utter chaos. Anchor it to your heart. It will tow you to safe harbor.

"Long time ago in a world now glossed over in foggy myth and fragmented legends, there dwelled King Minos and his wife Queen Pasiphae on the island of Crete. Due to some rather scandalous behavior on her part, there was born to her a monster child: half bull, half man. They called him the Minotaur. So voracious was his appetite for human flesh, he threw the inhabitants of Crete into utter panic. The king commanded an ingenious inventor, Daedalus, to construct a prison for his monstrous stepson, a labyrinth from which no one could escape.

"In order to pacify those on Crete, the king also ordered the neighboring islands and city states to provide the Minotaur with regular shipments of succulent young people. Thus, every nine years, Athens was forced to send seven young men and seven young maidens to feed the ravenous monster.

"Against his father's wishes, Theseus, son of the king of Athens, volunteered to be on the list. A dreamer of heroic adventures, he secretly planned to kill the Minotaur and return to Athens under the white sails of victory.

"Under the mournful black sails, the fourteen young Athenians left for Crete. When they arrived, King Minos threw them into a prison to await their gruesome fate. But Ariadne, one of the five beautiful daughters of King Minos and Queen Pasiphae, spied the handsome Theseus. She couldn't bear the thought that he'd be next on the Minotaur's dinner menu. Approaching Daedalus, she begged him for help.

"He handed her a ball of string and said, 'When it is midnight, take Theseus to the labyrinth's entrance. This ball of thread will roll before him and draw him deeper into the maze to where he'll find the Minotaur sound asleep. Hold onto your end of the thread, Ariadne, or Theseus will never discover the way back out.'

"Now, I know that it seems rather harsh for a sister to plot the murder of her bullish half-brother, but passion and treason often go hand in hand. She had fallen head over heels in love with Theseus. She begged him to marry her and take her to Athens, and to this plan he readily agreed. You must understand, dear ones, this man needed all the help he could get.

"At midnight, Ariadne set Theseus free and guided him to the maze's entrance. While firmly clutching one end of the thread in her hand, she placed the ball down on the ground. Unraveling, the stringy sphere rolled out, drawing Theseus down long, dark curving passages, up steep stairs, through hidden doors and mirrored hallways, and finally into the innermost lair where the beast lay sleeping. Theseus jumped upon the dozing Minotaur and strangled him with bare hands. Then picking up the thread, the young man slowly wound his way back through the labyrinth of dead ends, false hallways, and disorienting reflections. Every time he despaired and thought himself lost, a little tug on the line reminded him of Ariadne's constant faith. That was all he needed.

"When he finally arrived at the entrance, there she stood, holding to her end of the thread. Under the cover of darkness, the two of them freed the other young Athenians, stole away to their ship, and immediately set sail for Athens. Some say that Theseus married Ariadne that night on the ship, but I seriously doubt it. What princess in her right mind would give up her entitlement to a royal wedding?

"Passion holds to no reason. Enthralled by love's charms, Ariadne had chosen to abandon her home and family to spend the rest of her life by Theseus' side. On the trip toward Athens, the ship stopped at the island of Naxos. The young people disembarked to feast and rest. A joyous fatigue overtook Ariadne. She fell into a deep sleep of lovely dreams but awoke to a dreadful revelation. The sails of Theseus' boat were disappearing over the sea's low horizon. While she had slept, the Athenians had tiptoed off and left her on the rocks of Naxos. Ariadne let out a cry of utter forlorn. What had she done to deserve this treatment from her beloved Theseus?

"Some say that the god, Dionysus, had taken a liking to Ariadne and craved her for himself, that he had ordered the mortal Theseus to release her. But don't you believe that for a second. What really happened was that Theseus had dropped the ball. Wandering off into the maze of mirrors, basking in his own heroic reflections, he had lost the thread of what's important in life. Ariadne simply didn't fit into his mythic image of himself.

"After that, Theseus got downright stupid. He forgot to change the color of the ship's sails from black to white, so that when they entered the harbor of Athens, his father, thinking his son eaten, threw himself into the mortal sea. Later on, in another story, Theseus ended up trapped in Hades and the mighty Hercules had to rescue the dolt. Frankly, he should have left Theseus to rot in Hell. I tell you, without Ariadne, that man was a lost cause.

"Dear ones, I end this story with a single caution. Don't drop the ball. Don't let go of the thread, no matter what ego temptations you face. That thread, if you honor the gift of it, will always lead your heart home."

ONE

what is absence but a nothingness against which you cannot defend yourself? A lost love sailing off into the distance. A gnawing void that either swallows you, piece by piece, or teaches you the bitter lessons of endurance, hour by hour. In the short-shrift days and the cold, silent nights of New England, winter arrives to remind human beings of the power of deficiency and the poignancy of the sun's warmth.

At Two Cranberry Lane in Duxbury, Massachusetts, Harriet McWhinnie peered out the kitchen window at a world obscured by a cold, damp fog billowing in from the Atlantic Ocean. She could see nothing but an anxious reflection smirking back at her.

Good grief, what am I going to do?

An hour earlier, she had arrived home, ready to trumpet her new position at the State Street Bank in Boston. In one week's time, she would be handling institutional portfolios worth millions of dollars. A six figure salary to boot.

But even as she had opened the door to the rambling McWhinnie household, she could tell that something had gone terribly wrong. Upstairs, Luna was screaming at her twin sister Sola. "Don't ever come into my room again and touch my things."

"I didn't, you horrible person," yelled Sola, slamming shut a bedroom door.

At the top of the stairs posed Opal, Harriet's eighty-one-year-old mother, buck-naked, grinning at the fuss while clutching the hand of her wide-eyed, five-year-old grandson. Upon seeing his mother, Justin pulled free and clambered down the stairs. "Mommy, Mommy, that new lady ran away."

"Who, baby?"

"That new lady."

"Mrs. Schmuckal?"

At the top of the stairs appeared Luna. "Grandma, for God's sake, get some clothes on."

The old woman shook her head. "Don't want to."

"Mom, tell Grandma to get dressed. It's disgusting. What if one of my friends suddenly knocks on the door?"

"What happened to Mrs. Schmuckal? She's only been here three days. I thought surely she was—"

"Gone for good." Opal smiled, cupping her hand and waving her fingers, then added:

All the world's a stage
And all the men and women merely players;
They have their exits and entrances.

"'And one man in his time plays many parts.' I, too, remember my Shakespeare, Mom. But what happened to Mrs. Schmuckal?"

"Sola hit her," said Justin.

"What?" Sola was the sweetest, most gentle of all her children.

"Pray tell, dear, who is Mrs. Schmuckal?" asked Opal.

"The agency woman I hired."

Luna exited the hallway, only to return with a purple sheet which she draped over her grandmother.

"A toga," Opal exclaimed.

"What happened, Luna? Mrs. Schmuckal was supposed to be the answer to my prayers."

"God, Mom, you really know how to pick them. First, you imposed on us that Nazi Gertrude Hitler."

"Heller," Harriet corrected.

"Whatever. She thought by making us all eat her homemade candy, we'd come to love and obey her. Only Grandma and Justin fell for it. Then along came Prudence The Disaster, followed by Marian The Manipulator, then Crazy Caroline. Need I go on, Mother? Frankly, I'm glad that Sola hit her. After three days, Schmuckal's eyes were turning mean and squinty."

"Et tu, Brute," added Opal, flouncing the lavender sheet behind her.

Muffled sobs echoed from an upstairs bedroom.

Justin squeezed Harriet's hand. "Sola's crying again."

"I know, sweetie. Come on, let's help Grandma dress, so she doesn't catch her death of a cold. Then I'll go see what's bothering Sola. Luna, I want you to set the table, pull out the casserole from the freezer, and pop it into the oven. Okay?"

Luna groaned. "Why does everything always fall on me?"

"Because I need you to do this," Harriet answered.

"If you had only stayed with Dad—"

"Don't even go there, kiddo." Harriet's voice assumed its most menacing tone. "I need your help. We have to pull together, or else this family is going to fall apart."

Brushing past her, Luna muttered, "As if it hasn't already."

Harriet slumped down into a kitchen chair. No time to lose. She had only a few days in which to hire someone. Agency people had been drifting in and out of her house as if it were a shelter for the homeless. They'd stay a couple of months, then presto, say their quick goodbyes, unable to mask the relief on their departing faces. But Schmuckal's three-day stint set a new record.

Harriet required a person willing to hang in there, perhaps someone with a messianic or martyr's complex. She could handle the situations at night and on the weekends, but she desperately needed someone there during the day. To make sure that Opal didn't wander off. To pick up Justin at school and entertain him in the afternoon. And then there was the problem with Sola, her blond, sweet fifteen-year-old with a mild case of cerebral palsy, profound learning disabilities, and certain other peculiarities.

Luna could fend for herself, but it wouldn't be fair to ask her normal daughter to give up her own life to take care of family members.

No, Harriet had to hire someone and quickly. No more Agency people. But how to find the right person?

She picked up a pen to write an advertisement for the classified section of The Duxbury Clipper. Something eye-catching and to the point.

Help. I'm desperate.

A bit too dramatic. She scratched out the words.

Need a challenge? Excellent salary/benefits for a mature woman in daytime family care. Must be flexible, imaginative, and have a good sense of humor.

There, that should do it. No specifics to scare off potential applicants. She attached her phone number, then faxed it to the newspaper.

Harriet peered out the window into the early night settling over the seaside town. In a half-whisper, half-prayer, she murmured, "Who knows what will arrive on the next tide?"

Off in the distance, the foghorn hooted in ghostly rhythms, warning boats of impending doom if they approached too close.

TWO

After publication of the advertisement, Harriet had only two days left in which to interview people for the position. First in line was Mabel Makepeace, a solid chunk of a woman in her mid-forties. A mother of grown children, Mabel was looking for something to occupy her time and attention. "What a cute little boy," she said, watching Justin attach a string to a Lincoln log scaffolding which, to Harriet's mind, oddly resembled a set of gallows. "Is he the one whom I'll be watching?"

"Yes," said Harriet, "but there are also his twin sisters."

"Oh? Are they little tots too?"

"No, they're fifteen years old."

"Adolescents can be difficult, you know. Especially girls." Worry wrinkles flickered across Mabel's forehead.

She doesn't know the half of it, thought Harriet. "That's why I pay such a good salary."

"Do they fight a lot?"

"Yes. They're quite different from each other."

"I don't know." Mabel gritted her teeth. Her polite smile morphed into a quick grimace.

Harriet pushed herself off the living room chair. "It doesn't seem to me that you really enjoy adolescents."

"How much are you willing to pay?"

Harriet shook her head and opened the front door. "Thank you for coming by."

"Well," exclaimed Mrs. Makepeace, "if that's how you feel about it." She gathered up her pocketbook and raincoat and harrumphed out the door.

A young woman with a blond, bouncy pony tail and tie-dye cotton dress presented as the second applicant. "Hi, I'm April Showers," she said, vigorously pumping Harriet's hand. "It's the wrong name for me but that's when my parents, you know, conceived me under a pew at St. Michael's Catholic Church. Really, I've got a sunny personality. I'm not a water person at all but an air person. An indigo child. You know, lightness and laughter. You said you needed someone with a sense of humor. Well, most everything strikes me as funny. By the way, I love your house." Giggling, April swayed from one foot to the other. "See I warned you, didn't I?"

Harriet had only one question. "How old are you, April?"

"Going on twenty-five, although I know I look a lot younger. They say that's because laughter keeps you young." Her high-pitched voice both chortled and snorted.

Luna would strangle her the first chance she gets, mused Harriet. She ushered April Showers out into a grey, spitting rainstorm.

The third applicant, in a matching blue pantsuit and short, serious haircut, looked more promising. In her late forties, Mary Turner still retained youthful energy while having accumulated some life experience. There was a sense of calmness about her, almost bovine in nature, a solidity that Harriet found strangely comforting. Harriet described Justin's schedule, Opal's dementia, a bit on the twins, and was about to talk terms when Mary inquired, "Are they Christian?"

"Well, I guess so. I mean they've all been baptized."

"But do they take Our Lord Jesus seriously?"

"I'm not quite sure what you mean."

"Well, you said that your daughter, Sola, sometimes gets into screaming fits and uses foul language, for no reason at all."

"Yes, but—"

"And that your mother can take a notion to throw off all her clothes and wander around the house shamelessly."

"Sometimes—"

"And that you've caught your daughter, Luna, behind the woodpile smoking more than once."

"But don't you think—"

"That evil comes in many forms and disguises? I do. Now I can help clear up the mess here."

Harriet flinched at the word *mess.*

"But I will need the help of Our Lord and Savior," Mary continued, "and I can't do that without your help too." She reached over and grasped Harriet's hand, her eyes boring into Harriet's soul.

"What kind of help?" Harriet extracted her hand.

"First, it's important that children read the Bible everyday in order to cultivate the right values. Do they go to church?"

Harriet couldn't remember the last time. Justin's baptism? Luna had attended a bar mitzvah a few weeks back. Before moving into the McWhinnie household, Opal used to hold Crone/Earth Celebrations in her backyard during the full moon.

"There are other spiritual traditions besides Christianity," Harriet countered.

Mary shook her head. "The only way to Heaven is through Jesus Christ. If the children don't understand that, what's going to happen to them? I want to be clear about my philosophy of childcare, so that we understand each other perfectly."

"Oh, but I do," replied Harriet. She terminated the interview with as much Christian compassion as she could muster.

Only one person remained on the list of respondents. Harriet sighed, wishing she possessed the keen faith of a Mary Turner, for then she could trust in the Lord to take care of all her problems. But the only God she had ever known seemed content to let Harriet make all her own mistakes. If ever there was a time for prayer, this was it.

A firm knock on the door heralded the last applicant. Harriet checked the mirror to make sure that she looked presentable, trustworthy, and above all, calm. Serene as if any problem in the McWhinnie household was easily surmountable.

As she slowly opened the front door, the first pale rays of morning sunlight peeked out from behind the dense, dark ceiling of troubled clouds. Standing before her was a short, brown-skinned, black-haired woman, of mature age and muscular build, in black pants and burnt orange blouse. The woman extended a work-worn hand. "Hello, I'm Agatha Stands."

"Harriet McWhinnie. Won't you please come in?"

The woman gave a low whistle as she entered. "This is all yours?"

"Yes."

"It's huge."

Harriet guided her into the living room. "What kind of name is 'Stands?' Mexican?" Immediately, Harriet silently chided herself. *What a stupid question. Obviously 'Stands' is not an Hispanic name.*

"No. Indian."

"You come from India?"

"No. Indian, like in Cowboys and Indians."

"Ah, Native American then."

Agatha nodded.

Harriet devoutly believed in ethnic sensitivity.

"Are you married?" she asked the woman.

"Once upon a time—when I believed in fairy tales and that everything ends happily thereafter. What does Mr. McWhiny do?"

"It's McWhinnie, and he doesn't live here anymore. I'm divorced." Harriet looked away as if embarrassed by that revelation.

A smile warmed Agatha's face. "Some people say it's much better that way. Be your own person."

"I guess it depends on whom you ask. Would you like some tea?"

"Coffee—strong, black, and with three tablespoons of sugar, thank you."

While Harriet busied herself in the kitchen, Agatha trailed stubby fingers across the hard spines of books in the large, built-in, walnut bookcases. When Harriet returned, Agatha clucked in admiration. "You have a whole library's worth here."

"Reading is one of my favorite habits."

"Me too."

Harriet handed her the cup of coffee. "Let me tell you straight out what I am looking for."

Agatha sat down. "Good. I don't like it when people pussyfoot around."

Harriet cleared her throat. "I'll start with the youngest one, my baby Justin. He's five and attends kindergarten. Very bright and playful, an active boy. I need someone to pick him up after school and watch him in the afternoons."

"Okay."

"Then there are the twins, Sola and Luna. Luna, my brunette, is your typical teenager. Mouthy, grouchy, and full of herself. Other times, she can be very loving and sensitive."

"The moods of a young woman." Agatha nodded.

"Sola, my blond daughter, has some real problems."

"Like?"

"When she was born, there were a lot of things wrong with her. They said she was a failure-to-thrive infant. She possessed but one functioning kidney, a cleft palate, protruding ears, hearing loss, and a mild case of cerebral palsy with weakness on her left side. We later discovered that she suffers from profound learning disabilities, so she goes to a special high school. Despite the multiple operations in the past, she's often the most empathic of all my kids. Other times, she'll suddenly burst forth with wild accusations. I've taken her to lots of doctors, even to a psychiatrist, and frankly, no one really knows what the problem is."

"So that's it."

"Well, not completely. There's my eighty-one-year-old mother. A brilliant woman, she started becoming confused about two years ago, after my father died. The doctors told me that she has a form of dementia. I had a hard time believing it, but it soon became clear that she couldn't live alone. When my husband left—I mean when I asked my husband to leave—I brought her here to live with us."

"Are you sure there aren't any other skeletons in the closet?" Agatha smiled, seemingly unperturbed by all this information.

"Not that I can think of. Well, there's Digger. I've got him on a running line in the backyard."

"A dog, I hope."

"A Shetland sheepdog."

"They tend to be well-behaved. I used to raise them."

"Terrific," exclaimed Harriet. "Then you can help us with him as well. He's four years old and totally neurotic. When we put him outside, he attacks the door. When we bring him inside, he attacks the door."

Indeed, Agatha had observed claw marks scarring both sides of the front door. As she looked around, she could see that other doors had been equally brutalized.

"That's unusual for a Sheltie."

"When people try to leave the house, Digger will run circles around them, barking. He also careens around corners and tears down the stairs. If you're not careful, he'll cut your legs out from under you."

"Is he blind?"

Harriet shook her head. "No. Excitable, hyperactive, and with problems in applying the brakes."

"And he digs, I gather." A wry smile appeared on Agatha's face.

"Our back yard looks like a mine field. We yell at him a lot, but it doesn't do any good. Look, it's a lot to ask of one person, I know. Things can get really hectic around here. If it wasn't for my therapist and my job, I'd lose my sanity. I'm rather desperate for help."

What makes me be so honest with this woman? I'm going to scare her away, worried Harriet.

"Okay," said Agatha, draining her coffee cup. "I'll start today."

"Today?" Harriet was surprised. "But don't you have to get your affairs in order?"

"Haven't had an affair for a long time." Laugh lines crinkled around Agatha's brown eyes.

"I mean, I wasn't expecting someone to start until Monday."

"Today," said Agatha.

"Well, that's wonderful. Do you have any references?"

"Nope. Just me. My history is my own. I'm a private person. Now, if that's a deal-breaker, so be it. I also want to be paid in cash at the end of each week. No checks. No government forms."

"But what about Social Security taxes? As your employer, I need to declare how much I'm paying you."

"Look, it's better this way. As I told you, I'm a very private person. Don't want no government snooping on me. If you knew the history of my people, you'd understand."

"I'd be breaking the law," Harriet protested. *What to do? Either I hire her or stay at home and lose my job.*

"Right," said Harriet. "I guess we'll have to do it your way for now. What's your address, in case I need to reach you for a night or weekend duty?"

"I think right here would be a fine place to live."

That set Harriet back a second. She hadn't planned to hire live-in help, but immediately she could see its advantages. Winston's study on the third floor was no longer of use. There was a full bathroom up there as well. It would give Agatha a place to retreat when the day was done. Besides, what choice did she have?

"I'd require a year's commitment." Harriet hoped to forestall any immediate flight from the McWhinnie family chaos.

Agatha nodded. "I'll stay here as long as you need me. Not a minute more. Not a minute less."

A smile crept into Harriet's face. Little did Agatha Stands realize that she had just signed on for an eternity.

THREE

"May I help you with your bags?" asked Harriet.

From the front seat of an ancient pick-up truck, Agatha gathered up a lumpy, folded blanket bound by two leather strips. In the truck bed lay two battered suitcases, one tied together with string, one with duct tape, and a large, locked aluminum trunk. Together, they made several trips up to the third floor, hauling the luggage. Harriet noted the powerful strength in the woman's arms.

"I have this whole floor to myself?" Agatha asked.

"Is that okay?" Harriet lowered Winston's futon couch into the bed position.

"Absolutely." Agatha launched herself onto the thick mattress, testing it for firmness. "Perfect."

She got up and explored the attic area. "A bathroom to myself. Wonderful." Two windows, one facing east, the other west, framed the third floor of the large, Victorian home. To the north, an unfinished storage area, full of stacked boxes of Christmas ornaments, a pair of antique, porcelain dolls, old National Geographic magazines, Winston's childhood golf trophies, and Harriet's former hope chest.

Agatha opened one of her two suitcases and pulled out an assortment of tee shirts and jeans, cotton underwear, and multi-colored socks. "Now to find my good pair of pants."

A broad hint for Harriet to leave.

"You'll discover towels, sheets, everything you need in the bathroom closet. Let me know if I've forgotten anything."

"I will." Agatha softly closed the door.

An hour later, she reappeared downstairs in a pair of faded denims and a brown tee-shirt that featured the piercing, yellow eyes of a wolf. "I hope you didn't expect me to wear a uniform." She smiled.

Harriet didn't know what to say. The Agency people never dressed in uniforms, but then again, they didn't wear tee-shirts and jeans.

"Because uniforms slot people," continued Agatha.

"Okay," said Harriet, not wanting to ruffle any feathers at this delicate time in their relationship. "Help yourself to the sandwich fixings. Then I'll show you the route to Justin's school." She looked out the kitchen window near the driveway. "Is that truck safe?"

"It should be. It's got over one hundred and forty thousand miles on it."

That didn't bring Harriet much comfort. "Maybe we'll take my car. When on duty, you can drive my mother's car."

Having collected Justin and shown Agatha the route, Harriet left the two of them at home to get acquainted. "I've got to go grocery shopping. The girls will arrive later. On my way back, I'll pick up Mother from the Senior Day Care center."

Justin peered out his second story bedroom window as his mother drove off. He turned around and glanced at Agatha. "I build houses," he announced.

"I bet you do."

She helped him pull out a pile of interlocking wooden logs, then sat as Justin demonstrated how to construct a cabin.

"That's very good."

"I'll build a garage now."

"Okay."

She watched him erect a smaller enclosure, one with three sides. Justin then rummaged around in the back of his closet and emerged with two cars, one red, one blue. "This is a poor ship." He pointed to the red one. "Like the one Daddy has."

"And this?" Agatha picked up the blue car.

"That's a super roof. It should be black like Mommy's, but I don't have a black one."

"Then blue will do."

Justin took the toy car from her, then with one in each hand, he ran the cars round and round the log house. Sometimes, they crashed into each other with Justin amplifying the sound effects. He looked at her to see if she was as fascinated by the commotion as was he. But Agatha had pulled out a nail file from her pockets and was working on her cuticles. He parked the blue car in the garage and retired Daddy's car to the back of the closet, then wandered over to where Agatha was sitting.

He leaned against her ever so lightly, watching her smooth out the rough edges of her fingernails.

"You miss him, don't you?" she said, not looking at him.

His shoulders slumped, almost imperceptibly. "I don't have a car. I'm too young."

"But if you did, you'd be able to drive over to his house." Agatha put down her nail file. "So, you better let me teach you how to drive."

"How?" He looked quizzically into her face.

"Well, first you have to know how to handle the wheel. Here." She patted her ample lap and held out her arms, hands upon an imaginary wheel.

An invitation. He didn't know whether or not to hold back from the new babysitter. He placed a tentative hand upon her knee.

"BRRRRRRRRRR." With a rolling tongue, Agatha set the engine into motion. "All aboard."

He climbed into her lap, facing outward.

"Put up your hands to grab the wheel," she ordered. "Place them under mine."

Up they flew, soft little fists touching the palms of her callused hands.

"Now let's make this little baby zoom to the right." Hands working in unison, they jerked the imaginary wheel to the right, then to the left, their bodies pitching side to side as they took the street corners fast.

"BRRRRRRRRRR," he yelled. "Faster, faster."

"To the sea," said Agatha.

"To the mountains," shouted Justin.

"To wherever we want to go."

So far was their journey, so reckless in their demand for speed, that neither of them took notice of the dim afternoon sun disappearing behind the creeping shadows of dusk. Only when they heard the front door open and shut in succession, the voices of Harriet and her mother, the singing off-key by Sola, and the telephone monologue of Luna, did Agatha and Justin slow down, apply the brakes, and park their imaginations.

Trooping downstairs, Agatha spotted Harriet. "We got acquainted," she announced.

Justin ran and threw his arm around his mother's waist.

Standing beside Harriet in a red winter coat was an short, old woman with white hair and kind eyes.

"This is my mother, Opal McCarthy. Mother, this is Agatha Stands. She has come to live with us. She's replacing Mrs. Schmuckal."

"Who's Mrs. Schmuckal?" Opal asked.

"A grinch. Hi, I'm Luna, the only normal one around here." The grinning teenager reached out to give Agatha a firm handshake.

Agatha took Luna's hand and turned it over, palm up. Her finger traced the line around the thumb joint. "You're going to live a very long time," she said.

"Really?" Luna was all ears. "You read palms?"

Agatha nodded.

"Cool. So, how many lovers will I have?"

"Luna, behave," said Harriet, helping Opal out of her winter coat while Justin's arms clung to her middle.

Agatha rotated the hand to the area below the little finger. "You will have two great loves."

"Two? Awesome."

"Yes and no. It means that life will give you harsh losses as well as deep happiness." She gently dropped Luna's hand and turned her attention to the other teenager who was seated at the kitchen table.

"You must be Sola," said Agatha.

Sola looked up from the book she was reading.

Agatha was struck by the tremendous difference in the twins' appearances. Of small stature and short, curly blond hair, Sola possessed a shiny, translucent skin, a delicate, oval face curving down past pale blue eyes with sleepy lids and flat cheeks to an underdeveloped chin. In contrast to Sola's disproportionate features, Luna looked like a typical teenager, attractive and sullen at one and the same time, with fierce and penetrating brown eyes and long brown hair that fell straight over her shoulders. Sola's concave posture suggested a shy reclusiveness, whereas Luna's curvaceous carriage asserted itself, brash and bold in gesture.

"Hi." Sola spoke in a soft, high-pitched voice, glancing briefly at Agatha before returning to her book.

To Agatha, there was a pleading look behind those blue eyes. She touched the back of Sola's hand and whispered, "Don't be afraid. I walk in soft moccasins, in the sun dance way."

Sola's head jerked up in attention. Her eyes queried Agatha.

Agatha answered, "I know where I put my feet."

Opal sat down by Sola and wrapped her arms around the girl. "She's my special grandchild."

"I love you too, Grandma." Sola's head rested lightly on her grandmother's brittle shoulder.

Harriet doffed her coat and started unloading the bags of groceries. "So, let's get dinner going, kids. Sola, set the table.

Justin, unhook Digger from the line and bring him in for dinner. Luna, you can make the salad. Mom, I bet you'd like a glass of sherry, wouldn't you?"

"Of course, my dear."

"Me too," said Luna. "I'll pour the sherry."

"And stick your finger into each glass and lick it? No thank you. Agatha, would you like some sherry? It's the one thing that distinguishes us adults from the children."

Agatha shook her head. As Sola slid off the chair and limped over to the silverware drawer, Agatha offered her hand, but Sola needed no assistance.

"I can walk in my own way too," said Sola.

Except for Digger, everyone stayed in their best behavior at the dinner table. The mahogany-colored Shetland sheepdog prowled beneath the table, like a shark waiting for tidbits to drop. "Whatever hits the floor belongs to him," Harriet explained.

Harriet had outdone herself with steak tips, baked potatoes, crisp asparagus, and Caesar salad. It was time to celebrate her new promotion and the arrival of Agatha Stands. She placed Agatha in the middle, while positioning Opal and herself at opposite ends of the table. One after another, the kids bombarded the newcomer with questions.

"How old are you?" asked Justin.

"How old do you think I am?" Agatha's eyes sparkled.

"Twenty-five?" Holding an asparagus stalk in his hand, he licked off the butter.

Harriet laughed. "Now you can see why everyone loves him."

"No, really. How old are you?" pushed Luna, mashing the baked potato with a fork.

"Older than Methuselah," said Opal giving Agatha a wink.

"Are you older than Mom?" asked Sola.

"Because she's over the hill," added Luna.

"I'm fifty-eight years old," answered Agatha.

"Oooooo, that's ancient," exclaimed Luna.

"You don't look it. I thought you were in your forties," Sola said.

"Well, thank you, but I don't want to be in my forties. I like being fifty-eight. I'm at the age now when my people say a person might know something."

Digger's nose nudged Agatha's thigh. He placed his two front paws on one of her moccasins and pressed his full weight upon her foot. She reached down and grabbed him by the collar and gently but firmly pulled him out from under the table. "Sit," she commanded.

Digger wagged his tail, then plunged back under the table.

Once again, Agatha extracted the dog. This time she said, "Sit" and pushed his bottom down on the floor. Then she placed a flat hand in front of his nose and commanded, "Stay."

Digger's muscles twitched. His back legs inched upwards.

"Psst." With one finger she pointed at him.

Startled, he sat back on his haunches.

"Wow," said Luna. "And you didn't even have to yell at him."

"If I yelled, it would only fuel his excitement. Psst," she said again, as Digger began to move. "He has to stay there so that we can finish our dinner in peace."

"Agatha used to raise Shelties," explained Harriet.

"What should we call you?" asked Sola.

"Miz Stands will do, until you become an adult."

"I'm not a child," snorted Luna.

"You're not an adult either." Agatha served herself another helping of steak tips.

"That's what I keep telling her," echoed Harriet.

"So when do I become an adult?" Luna asked.

"You'll know. And when that time comes, you can call me Agatha, like your mother and grandmother." Agatha turned toward Opal. "Would it be all right if I called you Grandmother?"

Opal hunched her shoulders, as if anything Agatha requested would be okay.

"In my tribe, it's a term of respect for our elders," Agatha explained.

"How much Indian are you?" asked Sola.

"Honey, that's not polite to ask," cautioned Harriet.

"But people ask me all the time," answered Agatha. "We're the only people on this continent that get asked that question. What is your blood quantum? What makes you a real Indian: is it being a full-blood, a half-blood, a breed from the reservation?"

"I apologize for Sola's question," said Harriet.

Agatha held up her hand to show that she took no offense. "Sola, I had a mother who was half-Cherokee, half-black. I had a father who was half-Lakota, half-white. What does that make me? In my blood runs the history of this country. Some Lakotas say I'm a black person, a nigger. Some blacks tell me that I'm just a dirty savage. When I was your age, the white kids would call me Pocahontas in the winter and Aunt Jemima in the summer."

"Some of the neighborhood kids call me *Spazz*, because I have cerebral palsy," added Sola. "They don't want to hang around me." She eyed her sister, resentment simmering in her voice. "But they always want to be with Luna."

Luna looked away.

"Seconds anyone?" asked Harriet, picking up the salad bowl.

"I'm going to be a doctor," announced Justin.

"And heal the sick," added Opal.

"That's nice, sweetie." Harriet patted her son's head while passing the meat.

"So Sola," continued Agatha, "who tells you who you are and where you belong?"

"But didn't it make you mad when they called you names?" Sola persisted.

"Sure it did. I must have cried buckets of tears. Then somewhere along the line, I decided that no one could tell me who I was. I made up my mind that I belonged more to the First People. It had nothing to do with blood quantum. It had to do with what's in here." She tapped her heart area.

"Mom, what am I?" asked Sola, anguish in her voice.

"My beautiful daughter," answered Harriet.

"A freak," muttered Luna.

"My shishta," said Justin, his mouth full of asparagus.

"Someone very special," added Opal.

Agatha turned toward Sola. "So, you see, you're going to have to construct your own story."

F O U R

By Friday, the family had gotten to know Agatha well enough that she was no longer assaulted with questions at every meal. A routine began to develop. While Justin and the twins attended separate schools until mid-afternoon, the mornings in the McWhinnie home belonged to Agatha, Opal, and Digger.

Harriet suggested, "If you could take Mother out occasionally, drive around in her car, she'd really like that. To the grocery store and back, trips like that."

What a car it was: a luxury sport sedan with power meant for someone in their twenties. "An unscrupulous salesman sold Mother that car a couple of years ago. It didn't take her long to put dents on both sides of the front bumper. When she came here to live, I took away her keys." Harriet dropped the car keys onto Agatha's upturned palm.

Agatha had never before driven such a powerful car. The first time they came to a stoplight, she turned to Opal. "Grandmother, shall we see how fast it can go?"

Opal grinned.

Agatha revved the engine. As the light turned green, the car roared from zero to sixty miles per hour in mere seconds. "Jet propulsion," exclaimed Agatha. She removed her foot from the accelerator when the speedometer registered ninety miles per hour. She silently vowed she'd never take Opal riding in her ratty, old truck.

"My daughter won't let me drive anymore. I miss it. I can't go where I want to go," Opal complained. Obviously, it hadn't been a welcomed decision.

"We all come to that age when—"

"Usually because someone has had an accident. But I never did. Do you think that's fair?"

Agatha knew better than to be drawn into a conflict between mother and daughter. "I think it's hard to give up driving. Your daughter said you got lost one day when driving. Another time, you ended up going the wrong way on an eight-lane highway."

Opal shook her head. "No, that happened to someone else." But then her voice trailed off; her brow wrinkled as if she was recalling a similar experience. She stopped, then looked at Agatha. "What's wrong with me?"

"What do you mean?"

"I forget things. I keep losing my place . . . in this world."

"What did the doctors tell you?"

Opal's shoulders shrugged. "Nothing."

"What has your daughter told you?" The key question.

Opal's eyes grew sad. "She's become the parent now. Spends most of her time reassuring me, but I can tell something's not right."

"And you'd like to know?"

"Yes, I would," said Opal. "I've always preferred to be in the know."

"Okay," said Agatha. "I'll try to find out." She made a mental note to discuss this with Harriet. "In the meantime, Grandmother, I'm your personal chauffeur, your tour guide, and your partner in crime."

Grocery store visits, indeed. Agatha sensed that Opal was more open to adventure than Harriet fully appreciated. The mental impairment may have affected Opal's judgement, but she still retained good mobility and muscular strength for an octogenarian. They could have a lot of fun together.

That Friday turned out to be a chilly opportunity to visit Plymouth Rock. Agatha had never seen it. She expected to find a huge boulder, many stories high, on which the First People stood, watchful as the strange Pilgrim vessels sailed into the harbor.

Upon seeing the Rock for the first time, Agatha protested, "But it's tiny." No longer were people allowed to stand on it, having chipped away so many pieces that the Rock had diminished considerably in size.

Opal began laughing.

"What's so funny, Grandmother?"

"I remembered an old joke. It goes like this: What did one Indian say to another when they saw the Pilgrims arriving?"

Agatha shrugged her shoulders.

"'There goes the neighborhood.'" Opal grinned.

Agatha reached over and touched Opal's cheek. "Ain't that the truth." She looked at her watch. "Let's get some lunch. A deli sandwich?"

Opal shook her head. "A hot fudge sundae."

Not quite what the doctor or Harriet would order, but who cares? thought Agatha. *At eighty-one, a person ought to eat what they want to eat.*

One bare scoop of sugar-free vanilla ice-cream for Agatha's lunch. For Opal, sheer happiness: three scoops of butter pecan ice-cream heaped with chocolate sauce, whipped cream, and a red Maraschino cherry. She not only finished it in record time but licked clean the spoon.

In the late afternoon, Opal settled in for a winter's nap. Justin insisted that Agatha review his stalwart attempts to crayon within the lines of his coloring book. The telephone rang. Agatha got up from the floor to answer the phone.

"Hello, is Luna there?" A male voice.

"Who is calling, please?"

"Who are you?" The man's voice sounded suspicious.

"More to the point, who are you?" asked Agatha, not liking whomever was on the other end of the line.

"I'm her father," came the curt reply. "Now, can I talk to her?"

"Certainly. I'll get her." With a satisfactory clunk, Agatha dropped the receiver on the stone counter top, ambled to the bottom of the staircase, and yelled, "Luna, your father's on the phone."

"Daddy?" Sola's head popped out of her bedroom. She entered her mother's bedroom and grabbed the mobile phone. "Hi, Daddy. It's Sola."

"Hi darling. How are you doing? Is school going well?" Winston McWhinnie tried to keep the irritation out of his voice. He had only minutes to spare, and he needed to talk to Luna, not Sola. Sola could rattle on and on, unless he cut it short.

"I'm in a play."

"Really, that's great. Sola, do be a good girl and get your sister. Tell her I need to talk to her. I'm on the run right now. We'll talk later, you and I."

"Okay. I love you, Daddy."

"Me too." He heard Sola put down the phone and call out for her sister. He drummed his fingernails on his desk, as if that would hurry his other daughter.

Luna picked up the phone receiver. "Hi, Dad. What's up?"

"I got a great deal, hon. Three tickets for the Celtics game tomorrow night at the Garden."

"I'm not crazy about basketball."

"We'll do a little shopping downtown beforehand, go to an upscale restaurant, have ourselves a good time."

"Shopping?" That piqued her interest.

"As long as Justin doesn't fade out on us."

"Well, okay."

"Just one problem, though. There are too many steps down to our seats for Sola. You know how the stairs scare her. And I was only given three tickets, so will you tell her that in the near future we'll do something that she'd really enjoy?"

"Okay. She wouldn't want to come to a basketball game anyway." Luna knew that Sola didn't like jostling crowds impatient with her slow, awkward gait. *It's just as well*, she thought. *Only it's going to make Mom very angry.*

That was an understatement.

Harriet was furious. "No," she said, "Either all of you go with your Dad or none of you go."

"Mom," whined Luna, "that's not fair. Justin's never seen a Celtics game."

Justin grew real quiet, watching his sister and mother struggle over the weekend visitation.

"He'll survive," said Harriet, busily unpacking grocery bags on the kitchen counter.

"He promised to take us shopping as well and out to a good pizza palace." This latter statement was aimed at her little brother who loved pizza better than anything.

"Pizza?" Justin was all ears.

"No," said Harriet, but not quite as firmly.

Luna detected the subtle shift in her mother's voice. "He said that he'd do something special for Sola the next time. He felt really badly about it."

"I'm sure." Harriet tried to stifle the tone of sarcasm. She was a firm believer that children shouldn't suffer the angry dramas between divorced parents.

"He's right about the stairs, you know."

"Point taken, Luna. By God, you're going to grow up and be a lawyer like your father, the way you argue so."

"He's not a lawyer." Luna took up in his defense. "He's an important statesman, the Speaker of the House."

Harriet sighed. Winston had done a good job inculcating his children with his political reputation. "The difference between your mother and I," he used to tell them, "is that, in her job, she takes care of money matters whereas I have to respond to the needs of my many constituents. She uses her mind, but I have to rely on my heart as well."

When it came to Sola, Harriet couldn't fathom Winston's insensitivity.

"Okay. I'll take your grandmother and Sola to the movies tomorrow." It seemed to Harriet that she was always having to fill in the gaps for Winston.

"But please, please don't go to any movie you know I want to see," implored Luna. "C'mon Justin, we've got to pack." She grabbed her brother's hand and headed up the stairs.

Agatha entered the kitchen. "I couldn't help but overhear some of the conversation."

"I tell you, sometimes I want to kill that man." Harriet began dicing tomatoes. "I know the kids miss him, but I don't." Anger underscored her chopping motions. "He wants what he wants, not what others need."

"Sort of like Digger, huh?"

Harriet stepped back and gave Agatha an odd look. It was the first time she had ever heard anyone compare the powerful Speaker of the State House to a dog. But come to think of it, the analogy fit. Harriet nodded. "There are a lot of minefields where that man is concerned."

The paring knife slipped and nicked Harriet's finger. "See. The man still gets to me."

From the kitchen shelf, Agatha pulled down the band-aid box, extracted a bandage decorated with a Superman character, unwrapped it, and gently placed it over the Harriet's small wound. With her thumb, Agatha tested the metal blade. "You need a sharper knife."

"I swear, he's got his own supply of Kryptonite," continued Harriet. "And to think I used to get weak in the knees around him when we were first married. Funny how love and anger can produce the same reaction. I thought we were going to be married forever, like my parents."

"Your Mom wants to know why she's so forgetful these days." Better to talk about it now than later.

"I told her it's just old age."

"She knows it's not. She wants to know the medical diagnosis."

Harriet looked up from her salad fixings. "But would you honestly want to know? What if it were a death sentence, a steady path of deterioration? Would you really want to know?"

"She's not so far gone that she's quit being an adult."

Harriet's eyes began to tear up. She turned away from Agatha. "Oh, that will happen soon enough, believe me. The physicians said she's got Alzheimer's Disease. I don't have the heart to tell her. She knows only too well what that entails: the slow dissolution of all memory, all sense of self, control of bodily functions, until death becomes a relief not only to her but to the rest of us. How can I condemn her to that? I can't do it. I won't do it." Harriet dabbed at her eyes with a finger. "She's a wonderful mother and doesn't deserve what's going to happen to her."

Agatha placed a hand on the back of Harriet's shoulder. "It's a matter of honoring who she is and who she has been."

Harriet didn't say anything.

Agatha let her hand drop. "I'm on my way out for the weekend. I'll be back Sunday evening."

Harriet turned around. "Where are you going?"

Agatha didn't answer.

"Sorry, I shouldn't intrude on your private life. Have a good time, Agatha."

"I will." Agatha headed toward the kitchen door, bag in hand.

"One more thing," said Harriet.

"Yes."

"I want you to know how much I appreciate what you do here. You're a lifesaver to me."

"I know," said Agatha, softly closing the door.

F I V E

Sunday night, Luna and Justin arrived before Agatha. Their father dropped them off at the curb. "See you guys in a couple of weeks." He roared off in his Porsche, without noticing Sola emerge from the house, waving goodbye to him in his rearview mirror.

As he ran toward the front door, Justin dragged his overstuffed backpack on the ground. "I got something for you, Sola."

"What's that?" Sola bent down to receive his hug.

"Here." He shoved a green Celtics hat into her hands.

"Big deal," muttered Luna, lugging her suitcase up to the door. "You should see the clothes I bought on Newbury Street."

Sola adjusted the hat, a bit small for her, but she scrunched it down over her uncombed hair. "It's perfect," she announced.

As Luna edged by Sola, her bag snagged Sola's leg, sending her reeling off-balance. Justin's little hand flashed out to steady Sola.

"Sorry," muttered Luna.

"You did that on purpose," screamed Sola.

"I did not. Stop being so paranoid," yelled Luna.

"Play checkers with me." Justin tugged at Sola's hand.

"Why does she hate me so much?" asked Sola.

Digger flung himself upon Justin, licking his face and barking furiously. Joy overwhelmed the dog, his scattered flock of human sheep having returned to the fold.

"Shut up, Digger," yelled Sola.

Digger's bark grew more frantic.

Once inside the house, Sola slammed shut the front door which Digger then attacked.

"Stop it!" screamed Sola.

Yapping louder and louder, Digger jumped and scratched at the door.

Justin crouched down on the foyer floor and placed mittened hands over his ears.

Upstairs, Harriet could hear the commotion. Upon descending the stairway, she passed by Sola who was muttering to herself, "I do not smell bad. Just shut up, shut up, shut up."

"What, honey?"

But Sola didn't acknowledge her mother, so intent was she on stomping up the stairs.

Digger was still spinning in circles when Harriet got downstairs. She remembered what Agatha had said about being calm and in control. *I'm the alpha bitch here.*

Harriet grabbed the dog by the collar, thus halting Digger's manic motion. "Hush now," she said, placing her hand over his nose in the dominant position.

Justin stood up and came over. "Shush," he said to the dog, putting his finger up to his mouth.

"That's right. We're all becoming calm and quiet." She turned to Digger and ordered, "Sit." With a firm hand, she pushed down his quivering rear end. With a flat hand in front of his nose, she commanded, "Stay" and turned away from him.

"Stay, Digger," repeated Justin.

"What upset your sister?"

Justin shrugged his shoulders. "I gave her my Celtics cap."

Digger's ragged breathing began to slow down.

"That was a sweet thing to do. Did you have fun with your Dad?" Harriet tried to keep the tone of her voice neutral.

Justin nodded. "But I missed you and Grandma and Sola."

"What about Digger? Did you miss him?" Harriet looked askance at the Sheltie.

Justin's brow winkled. "Was Digger once Daddy's dog?"

Harriet nodded. "He thought it would be nice to have an animal around the house. Someone to greet him at the door, follow his every command, and lie down by his feet every night."

"Then why didn't he take Digger with him?"

"Because Digger turned out to be quite different than what he had expected."

Justin wrapped his arms around Digger's neck. "Mom, you won't ever send him away, will you?"

"No, darling. Digger is family. I may want to feed him to the wood chipper at times, but I'll never send him away."

Digger slurped his tongue over Justin's anxious face and looked up at Harriet with calm, loving, and oh so innocent eyes.

"Mom, you promised," whined Luna, entering into her mother's bedroom as Harriet sat trying to thread a needle.

"Where did I put my reading glasses?" Harriet's eyes scanned the room.

"You know that was a movie I've been dying to see."

"It was a great movie. Your grandmother and I especially enjoyed it. Sola liked the popcorn best of all."

"But why didn't you wait until I could see it too?" Luna stood there, hands on her hips, brow furrowed by the injustice of it all.

"You were at the Celtics game with your father." Harriet couldn't resist stating the obvious.

"Like I had a choice, Mom."

"Sola needs to have choices too, Luna. Your father decided to take only you and Justin. How do you think that made your sister feel? It's not like this is the first time this has happened. You come home with a new batch of expensive clothes, and he's bought nothing for her. Is that fair?" For the third time, Harriet licked and pinched the disobedient thread.

"Are you telling me that I should give her some of my clothes, Mom? Is that what you are saying?"

Harriet turned around to face her angry teenager. "All I know is that when you go off with your father, she feels left behind. But we had fun together this weekend. She was more outgoing with us. Then you return with all your gifts from him, and suddenly Sola retreats to her room, furious and saying things that don't make much sense."

"Mom, you don't understand Dad's position."

"Stop right there."

"No, hear me out. About a month ago, he took us all out to the pizza place. In the middle of eating a pizza, Sola suddenly yelled out that she didn't appreciate his trying to strangle her."

"What?" Harriet looked up, the thread dangling from her hand.

"Everybody in that place turned around and stared at him, like he was some kind of child abuser. I was there. Mom, it was crazy. He's never laid a hand on her or on any of us. But people are willing to believe anything, especially about politicians. What if a newspaper had run a story about it?"

Harriet could see the cold, hard logic of her daughter's argument. *Why hadn't Winston told her about this incident? He always did have the ability to deny troublesome facts in his personal life, lest he had to do something about it. He might be Speaker of the State House, but he was mute when it came to his own family.*

Even more disturbing to Harriet was the unavoidable conclusion:

Sola's behavior is getting worse.

SIX

December marched inexorably toward Christmas. The kids put up a tree and decorated it with old and new trinkets, flashing bulbs, strings of popcorn and cranberries from the nearby bogs, and a blond, cracked plastic angel blinking from the top branch. In the space of one week, two snowstorms had converted the seaside town of Duxbury into an old-fashioned New England winter scene. Snow mounded over the large boulders in Myles Standish Park, like whipped cream on apple brown betty. Ski tracks crisscrossed the forest roads. Hot cider, spiced with cinnamon, greeted the kids as they got home from school, ready for vacation.

Harriet retrieved her mother's gingerbread house molds from the basement and went to work. Justin and Opal especially enjoyed the routine of decorating the house with gumdrops and peppermint sticks. When nobody was looking, Opal broke off the gingerbread door and popped it into her mouth.

"Mom, somebody broke into the house," exclaimed Justin.

"Why so they did," said Harriet upon close examination. She peered at her mother whose cheeks were puffed out with incriminating evidence.

"A witch did it," he exclaimed.

Opal swallowed fast and furiously.

Agatha bent over to examine the damage. "That's the way it should be," she explained to Justin. "Now it's 'an open house.'"

Harriet reserved two weeks of holiday time to spend with the children. "Will you be here for Christmas?" she asked Agatha at the dinner table.

"No. I'll be gone until it's time to return."

"Where do you go on the weekends?" asked Luna. "Do you have a boyfriend?"

"Luna, that's not polite," cautioned her mother.

"Why aren't you spending Christmas with us?" asked Justin, his face dissolving into a pout.

"Where are you going?" asked Sola.

Harriet rolled her eyes. "I've lost all control here. Leave Agatha alone."

Opal intoned:

The woods are lovely, dark, and deep
But I have promises to keep,

Agatha smiled and recited:

And miles to go before I sleep,
And miles to go before I sleep.

Later, as Agatha helped Opal get ready for bed, she repeated the lines from Frost's poem, "Stopping By Woods On A

Snowy Evening." "You have an uncanny ability to say the right thing at the right time, Grandmother."

Opal touched Agatha's cheek with soft, tender fingers. "Sometimes I forget what I want to say. I remember, then poof, it's gone. Something's wrong up here." She tapped the top of her hoary head.

It was hard not to love this old woman with her sense of humor, her knowledge of literature, and her kindness. Agatha understood only too well Harriet's reluctance to speak the truth.

"Do you still want to know what's wrong, Grandmother?" She helped Opal climb into bed, then adjusted the blankets.

"Yes."

Agatha wished she had some way of sugar-coating the diagnosis. "The doctors told your daughter that you show signs of Alzheimer's Disease."

An almost imperceptible sigh issued from Opal's mouth. "Well," she said, pulling the blankets under her chin. "I guess that's that."

Agatha knew there was more, so she sat down on the side of Opal's bed and waited.

Opal looked at her quizzically. "Aren't you going to turn out the light?"

"Not yet," answered Agatha.

Opal's eyes took in all the old, familiar objects that she had brought from her former house. "You would have liked my husband, Edgar," she said. "Such a good man. Intense. Handsome. Sometimes difficult."

"Do you have a photograph of him?"

Opal looked perplexed. "I suppose Harriet does in one of her family albums. She's put together all the old family films on a DVD."

"Can we watch that tomorrow? I'd like to see what he looked like."

"So would I." Opal fingered her wedding ring.

"Grandmother, can I say something to you?"

She nodded.

"I admire the grace with which you've accepted the diagnosis of Alzheimer's Disease."

Opal looked thoughtful for a moment, picked up one of Agatha's rough hands. "Well," she said, "what choice do I have?"

Agatha could think of a lot of other reactions but nothing to match the wisdom of this old woman's heart. "I wish I could do something to change the outcome."

"You can." Opal smiled.

"Oh?"

"There'll come a time when I won't be able to direct my own life, assert my own will and wishes. I don't want to become a burden to my daughter. So when that time comes, Agatha, I have a big favor to ask of you."

Agatha held her breath.

"When I can no longer contribute in a meaningful way to this family, I want you to make sure that I go to a good nursing home. Harriet will resist that idea, but that's what I want. You understand?"

Agatha nodded.

"In fact, get a pen and paper, and I'll dictate my wishes. I'll sign and date it with you as my witness."

"Right now?"

"Now."

Opal sat up in bed. There was a fierceness to her command. Agatha retrieved a pad of paper and a pen and wrote down everything in Opal's words. Then she handed it to Opal to sign. Once that was done, Opal sighed contentedly and snuggled down under the blankets.

Agatha tore off the piece of paper, folded it, and placed it inside the top bureau drawer among Opal's tarnished jewelry and faded cotton handkerchiefs.

"There, that's done now," said Opal. She folded her hands atop the blanket, closed her eyes, and said, "Now, you can turn out the light."

The next morning, Agatha found the DVD of family movies and played it, much to everyone's delight. Sola shrieked, "There I am. I was only five at the time. Oh, look Luna, there's that red cowgirl hat you swore you'd wear forever."

"You remember the weirdest stuff," said Luna.

Grainy films of a reddish brown hue: shrieking little girls jumping about, a younger and thinner Harriet linked arm in arm with Winston, a running commentary by the seated grand-parents, Opal and Edgar, as they complimented the twins on their various activities. At one point, the camera caught Edgar leaning over and giving his wife a kiss, saying, "Darling, I'll love you forever."

In the film, Opal smiled and addressed the camera. "Forever is a very long time."

The old woman clapped her hands at seeing this segment.

Harriet leaned forward from the couch toward the television screen every time the film caught her with Winston. Brow

wrinkled, she wondered when and how things had turned sour
between them.

Seated on the floor, Justin kept saying, "But why aren't
there any movies of me?"

"Because you didn't exist, knucklehead," said Luna, tousling
his hair with her hand.

"I did too," he said, pushing away her hand.

"You weren't even a thought in Mother's brain," she
continued. It was fun to get a rise out of him. Justin was so
predictable.

"I was too," he exclaimed. "Wasn't I, Mommy?"

"Luna, stop teasing your brother," answered Harriet.

Luna loomed over her brother and pointed her finger at him.
"Now you're suffering from an existentialist crisis."

"No, I'm not! I'm not!" he yelled, bursting into tears and
running out the room.

"Sola, go up and check on your brother. Luna, you sit still.
You've caused enough trouble already." Harriet frowned at
her daughter.

Luna grinned.

As Christmas approached, Agatha prepared her pick-up for
the road trip. The kids knew better than to pester her about
where she was going. "Beyond the West Wind," was all she
would say. They hadn't the slightest idea what she meant.

At the breakfast table, she announced, "Time for me to go."
She fingered a large canvas bag.

"But I have a present for you," said Justin. He scrambled
to retrieve a crayon drawing of six stick figures and one
triangular character. "That's Digger," he announced.

"I'd have recognized him anywhere," said Agatha.

Harriet smiled.

"And who are these others?" Agatha asked, pointing to the stick figures.

"That's us," he answered. "There's Grandma, Mommy and Daddy, you, me."

"That makes only five," said Harriet.

"Someone's missing," sang out Luna, pointing at Sola.

"Yeah, that's Sola there," said Justin, touching the sixth stick figure.

Luna's face darkened. "You forgot me?"

Justin put this hand up to his mouth and anxiously looked around the family circle.

"Maybe you were out shopping," suggested Harriet.

"Thank you for the picture, Justin," said Agatha. "Now I have a present for you." She pulled out a large teddy bear from her canvas bag.

"Wow," he said, his eyes wide with delight.

"It's because you give such wonderful hugs, Justin. I told this bear that his job was to hug you back anytime you needed one."

Justin wrapped his arms fiercely around the bear, laying his head upon its furry chest.

"For you, Sola, I've made this present." Agatha reached into the bag and extracted a beaded set of soft moccasins.

"I didn't get you anything," Sola protested.

Agatha held up her hand. "These moccasins will carry you long distances but you need to take care of where you step."

Sola got up and threw her arms around Agatha, whispering, "I'm sure your family back home misses you. But while you're gone, we'll miss you too."

When Sola sat back down, Agatha pulled out a small jewelry box and handed it to Luna.

Luna's eyebrows shot up. Slowly, the teenager opened up the box, her forehead creasing as she extracted a square, silver brooch. On its mysterious face, an incandescent yellow moon lit a path across the dark blue, glistening water.

Harriet had never seen the likes of it. "What's the image made of? It's not a painted surface."

"Looks kind of old," said Luna, who didn't like antiques in any shape or form.

"It is old," said Agatha. "It shimmers because it's made of butterfly wings."

"Dead butterfly parts?" Luna scrunched up her nose.

"The butterfly is the medicine of transformation, Luna. You possess a powerful Anglo name, one whose meanings you should learn."

"McWhinnie?" she asked.

"That's just the half of it," said Harriet.

"Thank you," said Luna in a mechanical voice. "I'm sure I'll wear it someday." She deposited it on the table. It hadn't occurred to her to get a present for Agatha. After all, hadn't her father referred to Agatha as "the hired help?"

Harriet, on the other hand, handed Agatha a Christmas card containing a hefty bonus check.

Agatha caught her breath when she saw the amount. "That will be very helpful. Of course, I didn't forget you." She reached down into the her bag and pulled out a set of sharp knives.

"Oh my," said Harriet.

"All the better to cut away the fat and gristle," said Agatha.

A knowing look passed between them.

"I'll try not to wound myself," said Harriet.

"As for Digger, I have two gifts." She produced a large meat bone and a small clicker. "All the better for his training," she explained. Digger's nose sniffed the air.

Justin let him out the back door into the yard, bone in his mouth.

"One last gift," announced Agatha. "For Grandmother."

Opal sat up like a queen ready to receive the tribute of her subjects. It was the only gift that Agatha had wrapped in paper and ribbon. Opal gleefully yanked off the ribbon and paper, uncovering a rectangular metal object. She looked at it, then gave it a kiss.

"What is it, Grandma?" asked Sola.

"Lemme see, lemme see," begged Justin.

Opal rotated the gift so they all could see: an enlarged picture of Edgar in a metal frame.

"There's a button at the bottom. Push it, Mom," said Harriet.

Justin, however, did it for her. From the base of the photograph boomed Edgar's voice. "Darling, I'll love you forever."

To which everyone at the table answered, "Forever is a very long time."

SEVEN

Despite all of Harriet's best laid plans, the Christmas vacation was turning into an utter disaster. Distracted with making breakfast and chasing Digger out into the back yard, Harriet didn't get upstairs in time to help her mother dress.

Opal had decided she could do it by herself, but the old woman lost her balance and fell, slamming her head against the bureau as she went down.

Justin sounded the alarm. "Mom, I heard a crash upstairs."

"Oh, my God." Harriet took the stairs two by two. Her half-dressed mother was laying on the floor, eyes closed, bleeding like a stuck pig. "Mom, are you okay?" She grabbed a towel and applied pressure to the gash on Opal's forehead.

Opal blinked.

Thank you, God, she's still alive. Harriet allowed herself to breathe.

Sola appeared in the doorway. "What's wrong?"

"Get me a wet washcloth, darling," said Harriet. She stroked her mother's cheek.

Opal managed a wry smile and opened her eyes. "I fell and I can't get up."

"Just stay put."

Sola appeared with the wet cloth. Harriet wiped off the blood and, to her relief, saw that it wasn't a life-threatening wound. Still, she would need to take her mother to the Sykes Memorial Emergency Room in Plymouth for stitches.

"Do you think you can stand up with my help?"

"I can try. I don't think anything is broken."

Sola came over on her grandmother's left side. It was a juggling act for her to maintain her own precarious balance as she helped her mother lift up her grandmother.

"Now, let's get you fully dressed, Mother. I'm taking you to the hospital."

"No, that's not necessary. I'll be fine," said Opal holding the damp washcloth to her head. "I'm just a bit shaken up. Let me lie down, take a nap."

"I don't think so, Mom. C'mon, let's get you ready."

Sola helped her mother dress Opal in a pair of warm pants, socks, and shoes.

"Sola, come with me to the hospital. Tell your sister I want her to feed Justin breakfast and watch him while we're gone."

A few minutes later, a sleepy-eyed Luna appeared in a shaggy bathrobe and slippers. "But I told my friends I'd meet them downtown this morning. Grandma, you going to be okay?"

Opal smiled. "Miles to go before I sleep."

Harriet knelt down to tie her mother's shoelaces. "Luna, you have two choices. Either you stay here with your little brother or take him with you."

"Are you kidding?" The idea of being shadowed by her baby brother was ridiculous. "Okay, I'll call them. I'll meet them later." Luna reached into her bathrobe pocket, pulled out a cell phone, and opened the lid.

"Where did you get that?" asked Sola. Mom hadn't yet acquiesced to their demands for cell phones.

"Dad." Luna dialed a number.

Harriet struggled to her feet.

"Hey Judy," said Luna, "Something's come up. Can't meet you downtown. Check with you later." She flipped the lid.

"I thought we'd already discussed cell phones," said Harriet.

"You said it was too expensive, but Dad's agreed to pay for it. Besides, everybody has one."

"I don't," said Sola.

"What if you need me for an emergency, Mom? This way you can always reach me or I can reach you."

"Sola, get your grandmother's winter jacket. Luna, I worry about you getting brain cancer from the radio frequencies. Kids walk around all day with those things attached to their ears."

"Like umbilical cords," offered Opal.

"A bit higher, Mom," said Harriet.

"Would it make you happier if I got ear phones?" Luna counted on her mother's refusal to address the issue about her father's interference.

Harriet sighed. "Yes."

"Done," said Luna. "I'll pick some up today when I go shopping with my friends."

Sola reappeared with her grandmother's jacket. The two of them bundled Opal into the car. She looked like a sheik with her head wrapped in a white towel.

At the hospital, the young physician cleaned the cut, put in a few stitches, and took X-rays. He manipulated her neck, to which Opal responded with "Ouch, that hurts."

"She's going to have a stiff neck," he said. "She may have aggravated some arthritis. Keep an eye on her for the next few days."

For the next few days, thought Harriet. *How about for the next few years?* Harriet knew that for most Alzheimer's patients, the death sentence was seven years from the time of the initial diagnosis.

On the drive home, they were all quiet, until the car dipped in and out of a pothole.

"Ouch," said Opal. "Slower, please."

"Mom, can I have a cell phone?" asked Sola.

"Ask your father, darling. He's the one who seems willing to pay the price." Harriet's jaw tightened in silent protest.

"I'll ask him for a biography instead," Sola said. She thought that would please her mother and grandmother, both of whom believed in the companionship of books.

"I swear, Sola," her father once told her, "You're just like them. You'd prefer a book to a boyfriend." She knew he was simply teasing her, but the truth was, no boy had ever expressed any interest in her.

Books didn't care how she looked, talked, or walked.

Except for the mild cerebral palsy, sometimes Sola seemed almost normal. She read a lot over the Christmas vacation, especially biographies of beautiful, healthy women. But when her monthly cycle arrived, it was as if another force took over, sending her spiraling down into a period of dark suspicion, frantic anxiety, compulsive behavior, and crazy talk. The only thing that seemed to give her any peace was to don head phones and play Broadway musicals at volume pitch, as if to drown out all conversation.

Once more, Harriet drove to the hospital, as she had done many times before, to ask the simple question: "What is wrong with my daughter?"

The local psychiatrists interviewed her, rubbed their bearded chins, and offered a panoply of diagnoses, all of which Harriet had seen before: *Paranoid Schizophrenia, Obsessive-Compulsive Disorder, Panic Disorder, Generalized Anxiety Disorder, Atypical Psychosis.* Harriet did her homework and knew that none of them adequately described her frail, tortured daughter.

As she had for the previous three years, Sola dutifully attended psychotherapy every week. For the most part, she seemed to enjoy the special attention, but as far as Harriet was concerned, nothing fundamental changed. Their physician kept juggling a different regimen of drugs, most of which were sedating in nature. But Harriet refused to let her daughter sleep through adolescence, so she moderated the amounts she gave Sola, based on the girl's level of anxiety and dysfunctional behavior.

Beset by menstrual cramps and shifting hormones one late night, Sola got to screaming. "Shut up, shut up, shut up!"

Harriet jumped out of bed and hurried to Sola's bedroom. The light was out, and there was no one in the room beside her daughter.

Harriet turned on the light. "Sola, what's the matter?"

"They tell me I'm bad. That I'm not a girl, that I'm a boy. I'm not!" she yelled.

"Shush, you'll wake up the whole household, darling. Who is telling you that you're bad? Kids at school?"

Sola dissolved into tears. "No. I'm a girl, Mommy."

Harriet perched on the side of the bed and held her slight, trembling daughter. "Of course, you're a girl."

"They tell me I smell bad."

"Who?" Harriet was confused.

A look of pure anguish came into Sola's eyes. "The voices."

"What voices?"

Sola didn't answer for a moment, then grabbed her head and yelled, "Shut up!"

"These are voices in your head then?"

"They tell me I need to die. I don't want to die, Mommy. Don't let them kill me."

Oh, God, my poor, poor Sola. Her mind has turned against her. Harriet hugged her harder. "No one is going to kill you, Sola. But there's something wrong, and we've all failed you in finding out what it is."

"Can't you stop them? I don't want to live like this, Mommy. Please," she begged.

Harriet went to the medicine cabinet and got out one of the sedating pills to give her daughter. *It will silence those goddamn voices. It will help her sleep.* But Harriet knew it was simply a stopgap measure. She had never felt more helpless.

Luna tried to stay away as much as possible. She didn't want to be saddled over Christmas vacation with Justin,

Grandma, or Sola. "The whole place is nuts," she told her friends. "You wouldn't believe it."

Luna came to the conclusion that it might be advantageous if she could move in with her father. After all, didn't her father call her "My Princess" and shower her with gifts? She could cook for him, do some of the cleaning of his apartment. The only hitch was that she would have to transfer schools and leave her friends behind. Maybe she could persuade him to give her a car on her sixteenth birthday. That way, she could drive herself from Boston to the high school in Duxbury.

After persuading a friend, Jeffrey Porter, to give her a lift to her dad's Boston apartment late one afternoon, Luna lied to her mother. "I'm staying over at Judy's house."

Mom would have a conniption fit if she knew I was doing this, especially since she's never met Jeffrey. Luna felt a bit guilty, not so much about lying to her mother but about Jeffrey. He had a crush on her that was totally unreciprocated. *But how else am I going to surprise Dad?*

"Wait right here," she said to him outside of the Beacon Hill apartment building. "Let me first see if my dad's there."

She pushed the outside button, announced her name into a brass speaker, and waited for the buzzer to unlock the front door. When it sounded, Luna gave Jeffrey a thumbs up, before disappearing inside, riding the clunky, old-fashioned elevator to the third floor where she finally knocked upon her father's door.

To Luna's surprise, a tall, elegant young woman with red hair opened the door. "So, you're Winnie's daughter," the woman exclaimed. "C'mon in."

"Who are you?" asked Luna. "Is Dad here?"

"No, he's at a political shindig in Chinatown. He won't be home until late tonight. I'm Caitlin. I've been an aide in your dad's office for several years. Heard a lot about you. Would you like something to drink?"

Luna nodded. She looked around the apartment. It had been almost two weeks since she had last been there. Somehow, it all looked different, rearranged.

Caitlin returned from the kitchen bearing a glass of wild cherry soda. She handed it to Luna. "What do you think? Do you like it?"

Luna knew she wasn't talking about the drink. "It's not the same."

Caitlin laughed. "It's a lot more feminine. Your father knows nothing about interior decoration. I had to pack up some of his doodads to make room for my things."

"Oh," said Luna, suddenly getting the picture.

"He didn't tell you, did he? Just like a man. I moved in ten days ago."

"So you're roommates then?"

Caitlin smiled. "In a manner of speaking, yes."

She gave Luna a tour of the transformed two bedroom apartment. Certainly cleaner, no dirty socks littering the floor, and fresh, cut yellow flowers arranged in a clear blue vase on the dining room table. Luna couldn't help but notice that the only rumpled sheets were on her father's king-sized bed. The twin beds in the second bedroom remained untouched.

Luna finished off her glass of soda. "I have a friend downstairs waiting for me, so I've got to go."

"Okay." Caitlin seemed disappointed by the quick goodbye. "I'll tell your Dad that you dropped by."

Luna shook her head. "No. It's of no consequence. He'll just be disappointed that I didn't stay longer."

Luna had fully intended to keep Caitlin's presence in her father's apartment a secret from her mother, but it really bothered her. She took Sola into her confidence. "Can you believe that? She's only a few years older than us."

"Do you think he loves her?" asked Sola.

"Who knows? She's pretty, if you like redheads with freckles on their noses."

Sola peered into the bathroom mirror. "I've got freckles."

"She seemed nice enough, but I don't want to have to share him during our weekend visits, do you?"

"Where would she sleep?" asked Sola.

Luna rolled her eyes. "Where do you think?"

"Oh," said Sola.

Sola didn't know what to do with all this spicy gossip about her father, so she told her grandmother. "Luna thinks it would make Mom really angry if she knew."

"I bet," said Opal. *But Winston is a free man and men don't tend to stay free for long. Still*, she thought, *Harriet ought to know about it.* So Opal whispered into Justin's ear, "I'll tell you a secret. Next time you go stay with your Daddy, you'll get to meet his new roommate, Caitlin."

Justin promptly reported to his mother. "There's a girl living with Daddy."

"No," Harriet said. "He's got a girl who comes in and cleans for him."

"Her name is Caitlin, and Grandma says she's his roommate."

Harriet's eyebrows practically collided. "Your grandmother told you that?"

"Uh-huh." Justin puffed up as the Bearer of Important News.

Fortified with a glass of Tennessee whiskey, Harriet finally found a solitary moment. She retreated into her bedroom and dialed Winston's telephone number.

"Hello." A lilting female voice.

She sounds so young, thought Harriet. "Is Winston there?"

"Who's calling?"

"His ex."

"Oh, okay. Winnie, the phone is for you."

Winnie, like Winnie the Pooh? Harriet couldn't help smirking. She took another sip of whiskey.

"Hi, Harriet." His voice was guarded, girded for battle.

"You could have told me."

"About Caitlin? I meant to, but you know how busy I am. It slipped my mind."

"There's been a lot of slipping and sliding lately."

"What now?" He sounded tired.

"You gave Luna a cell phone."

"So? She needed one. That way I can keep in contact with her. Or do you object to that as well? God, Harriet, you're becoming a shrew." He paused. "I apologize. I'm sorry I said that, but the fact remains that I'm also her parent."

"Oh, Winston." Harriet was determined not to break down on the phone. "You are also Sola's father."

"And Justin's," he added.

"Do you care about what is happening with her? Do you even see her enough to know what is going on?"

"Luna tells me that Sola's been having a real hard time of it lately, that you've taken her to several medical appointments. I'm sure if the doctors had anything new to offer, you'd have shared that with me. Now if you have something of substance to report about her, I'm all ears."

"Otherwise don't bother me—is that it?"

"Harriet, sarcasm isn't going to solve anything. Now, if you need more money. . . ."

What I need is time. What I need is a life, she thought.

"No," she said. "You're of no use to me."

Harriet hung up the phone. She stood up and examined herself in the large mirror over the bureau. A tired, middle-aged face stared back at her. She smiled and finished the glass of whiskey. "At least, I kept my dignity." It was no small comfort.

From the bedroom wall, Harriet took down a photograph of a younger, newly-elected Winston standing proudly before the Massachusetts State House. Carefully, she detached the photograph from its moorings. In the sewing table, she retrieved her best scissors. The first cut slashed Winston's neck in two; the second performed open heart surgery on him; and the third obliterated his manhood. Harriet let the remaining fragments of Winston flutter into the wastepaper basket.

There, that feels much, much better.

Only now her glass sat totally empty.

EIGHT

Work is my salvation; work is my salvation. Toward the end of the holidays, Harriet kept her sanity by reciting this mantra.

About the time Harriet feared she was totally losing her wits, Agatha returned.

As her truck rattled around the corner onto Cranberry Lane, Agatha saw Opal standing out by the road without a jacket, arm flapping in the chilly air, a clutch of envelopes in her hand.

"What the—" Agatha screeched to a stop and rolled down the window. "Grandmother, what are you doing outside?"

"Helping Harriet," she answered, her eyes searching for other vehicles. "She paid her bills this morning. I'm trying to find someone." Her eyes clouded, her brow furrowed in confusion.

"The mailman?"

"Yes, that's it. Have you seen him? His name is Douglas. Nice man."

"I'll tell you what. I'll run these envelopes down to the post office after I get you inside. Okay?" Agatha parked the truck and escorted the shivering old woman into the house, just as Harriet was coming down the stairs.

"Agatha, I'm glad you're back. Mom, I've been looking all over for you."

Agatha nodded her head toward Opal. "She was outside, trying to flag down cars to take your paid bills to the post office. I told her I'd do it instead."

"I thought," said Opal, "that Douglas would come. . . ."

"Mom, Douglas was your postman twenty years ago. He doesn't work in Duxbury. I told you not to go outside by yourself." Harriet tried to keep frustration from honing an edge to her voice.

"I wanted to help," Opal said, her frail shoulders sagging in defeat.

"And you did," said Agatha, "because here I am. Now, I'll run them down to the post office."

"No," said Harriet. "That's my job." She threw on her winter jacket. "I could do with some fresh air. Besides, I need to get out of this house."

Agatha turned toward Opal. "I'll bring in my suitcase. Then would you like some hot cocoa?"

"With whipped cream?" suggested the old woman.

Agatha was quick to notice that Digger had reverted to his old behavior of attacking doors, shepherding people, and barking incessantly.

"Yap, yap, yap. You're back, back, back," he yipped, jumping up on her.

"Missed me?" asked Agatha, gently pushing him down. "Time to start your training again."

Every time she let him out, Agatha positioned herself between the door and the dog. Digger was confused. How could he hurl himself at the door with that human being running interference? Every time he barked, she made him lie down. Every time someone tried to leave the house, she put him on a short leash and made him sit. A contest of wills, and the human being seemed to be winning.

"You need a job," she said to him.

"Do you really think he understands you?" asked Luna.

"Oh yes. Maybe not the words, but he's watching my body all the time, listening to the tone of my voice. Here, I'll show you something. Bend over and place your wrist on your butt."

"You're weird." But curious, Luna complied.

"Okay, now wag your hand back and forth, side to side. That's right."

"Do you want me to say woof, woof too?" Luna laughed.

"Now wag your hand and point your nose at Digger."

Sure enough, the dog's tail began to thump in response.

"He thinks I'm a dog." Luna straightened right on up.

"No, he knows you're not, but he thinks you're finally getting smart enough to talk in his language."

"Cool." Luna repeated the experiment to the same satisfaction.

Agatha continued, "Among my people, his language has as much validity as those of the two-leggeds. Dogs, cats, wolves, bears, deer, raccoons—we're all part of the same Creation. They're our brother and sister nations. We're part of Digger's pack, and he needs to find his place in this pack. Otherwise, he'll keep on trying to take control. He needs a job."

"Like fetching a newspaper? He'd probably chew it up before it ever got to the table."

"Let's look at his assets. He's a good watchdog with a really deep, threatening bark," said Agatha.

"He digs holes. Maybe he could help Mom when she's planting flowers in the Spring."

In unison, they both shook their heads.

"He herds people," said Agatha.

"Keeps them from wandering off." An idea was beginning to form in Luna's brain. "Like Grandma."

"Very good, Luna. But we'll need to teach him that she is his sole sheep, to be a bit more selective."

"He's fast on his feet, lots of energy."

"Too much energy, don't you think?"

Luna nodded.

"I've got an idea. How about when I'm off work tonight, Digger, you, and I take a little trip?"

"Where to? Mom won't let us throw him off the pier."

"Only in your wildest dreams. It's a surprise. Wear sneakers and jeans."

"Okay." Luna loved mysterious challenges. She let it slip to the others that she and Agatha were going on a secret trip that night. Just the two of them.

"I wanna' go," howled Justin.

"Me too," added Opal.

Agatha held up her hand and said, "Maybe in a few weeks, but not tonight. Only Luna, myself, and Digger."

"Digger?" Justin shook his head.

"Luna didn't mention him," said Opal.

"He's the star of the whole show," said Agatha.

Harriet arrived home exhausted, yet revived by the return to work. The rules of investment, the hierarchy of the bank and its policies, the needs and goals of investors, possessed a predictable logic, quite contrary to the demands and whims of individual family members.

Agatha whispered in her ear.

"Luna?" she said, surprise etched in her voice. "You're a magician, Agatha Stands. Certainly, you have my permission." She wrote out and signed a check for one hundred and twenty dollars, then handed it to Agatha.

"That'll cover six weeks," said Agatha.

Before tackling dinner, Harriet retreated into the sitting room and her computer. Still smarting from Winston's unkind "shrew" remark, she summoned up an internet dating service and read the home page. *I can do this.*

They required a photograph of her, some vital statistics, a description of her personality and that of a desired companion. Was she interested in men or women? Harriet checked "men." Age range? Harriet wasn't interested in any boy toy, but she wasn't against dating someone a few years younger than herself. She wrote down "thirty-five" but couldn't decide on an upper limit, so left that blank.

How to describe herself?

"Attractive, medium height, well-rounded," she typed. *Maybe they'll think that last adjective applies to my personality and not to my body.*

"Fun-loving, successful professional woman," she continued. *The men will think I'm rich, but at least it'll weed out those scared of strong women.*

"**Pragmatic yet loves surprises. Open to long-term relationships. No game playing, please,**" she added. *I sound pathetic,* she thought. *Desperate.*

She checked off having three children living at home. *That should terrify most of them. At least, I don't have to mention Mother.*

What are the personality characteristics she is searching for in a man?

"**An affectionate, romantic man, twinkle in his eye, healthy, who loves laughter, music, books, and long walks on the beach,**" she answered. *I sound like every other woman in this world. Hello, I'm Harriet. Can anyone see through all this to the real me?*

Despite all her doubts, Harriet agreed to the conditions, gave the company her credit card number, and appended a flattering photograph of herself, ten years earlier and fifteen pounds lighter. She hit *Enter*, consigning herself to the wild, wacky world of the Internet.

After dinner, Agatha drove Luna and Digger to a large warehouse. During the whole trip, Digger thrashed around in the back seat while loudly barking into Agatha's ear. Outside the warehouse sat several vans and trucks loaded with dog crates. From inside issued the cacophony of excited woofs, arfs, yips, and yaps. Digger's ears shot up, but the tail tucked down.

"See, he's curious and yet afraid," said Agatha, attaching a leash to the dog's collar. She handed Luna a small bag of doggie treats.

"What's that for?" the teenager asked.

Nose to the ground, Digger trailed Agatha into the building. Lit up inside, the warehouse contained a front office and two large arenas—one for obedience training, one for agility training. In the latter area stood a course of plastic jumps, an eight foot A-frame, a see-saw, a set of twelve weave poles, and two plastic tunnels. Agatha handed the leash to Luna.

"I want to sign them up for a six week beginner's agility class," she told the bespectacled receptionist.

"Can she sit, stay, lie down, and come on command?" asked the receptionist.

"I hope you mean the dog," said Luna, leaning over the counter. "It's a he and his name is Digger."

"Yes," said Agatha. "He's able to perform all those commands."

"Can she run?" The woman looked over her glasses at Luna.

"Can a polar bear pee on ice?" Agatha winked at Luna.

Luna stood up straighter.

For the next hour, as Agatha leaned across the arena barriers, she watched Luna and seven other dog handlers learn how to run the dogs over jumps and through tunnels. All novices, the dogs initially shied away from the tunnels' dark interiors. Eventually the coaxing voices of their humans and the smell of treats pulled them through. Some of the dogs were natural jumpers, while others scooted under or around the jumps. Digger's attention never wavered. Once he knew what Luna wanted, he dashed through tunnels and hurtled over jumps with a speed that put other dogs to shame. When he finished each task, he'd strut toward Luna, tail held high.

Luna could not resist the infectious sense of triumph. She lavished the dog with cooing words of praise for his prowess, burying her hands into his fur.

In response, he licked her face and danced around her feet. At the end of the hour, both dog and teenager were exhausted by the demands of the agility course.

"That was so cool," Luna exclaimed as they left the arena. "Did you see how fast he was? He was the best one there, don't you think?" She turned from Agatha, bent down, and kissed the dog on his wet nose.

Digger slept the whole way home.

Every weekday morning, Agatha scoured *The Boston Globe* in search of things to do with Opal, adventures to stimulate her mind or her body. Opal's neck continued to ache and stiffen, so Harriet instructed Agatha to drive her mother to a masseuse who gently stretched the neck muscles. Still, Opal complained every time the car hit a bump or a pot hole.

Next, Harriet located a female Reiki healer who relied on the power of touch and energy to focus on Opal's arthritic neck. In one session, Opal's neck increased in range of motion. In two sessions, the pain completely disappeared. "I don't know what she does. I don't understand it," Opal told Agatha, "but I sure like it."

Between weekly Reiki sessions and massages, Agatha explored the coastal towns with Opal, stopping off for seafood lunches, local sights, and stores of seaside whatnots. Sometimes they would happen upon a musical event, a hidden museum, a display of historical artifacts. Opal's deep knowledge of history matched her love for literature. At night, Agatha would read books suggested by the old woman.

"Today," she said to Opal, "There's nothing of particular interest in the paper. Let's do something entirely different."

"What?" asked Opal.

"You'll see."

They drove to the Plymouth District Court, a large brick building with an imposing facade.

"Are you in some kind of trouble?" asked Opal.

"Nope." Agatha cautiously opened the door to a courtroom filled with people. She whispered to Opal. "We're going to watch a murder trial. It'll be better than the soap operas."

"Everybody rise," ordered the bailiff as the judge entered the room.

Opal struggled to her feet, but the judge waved her to sit down. "You can stay seated."

Five days in a row, Opal and Agatha attended the trial. Over dinner every night, she'd ask Agatha to summarize the day's proceedings for the family members.

"It's a case that pits brother against brother, son against father," explained Agatha. "What started out as a simple robbery of a convenience store turned violent when the store clerk refused to hand over the money. Instead, he whipped out a baseball bat and thwacked the masked gunman. In the struggle that followed, the gun went off and killed the young clerk. The robber took off running."

"What the bad guy didn't realize," added Opal, "was that the store had a video camera that caught all the action."

"But he was masked, right?" asked Luna.

"Right," said Agatha, "No one could identify the suspect. So they showed the robbery on the television news broadcasts the next night."

"I think I remember this case," said Harriet. "Didn't the robber have two adult sons who recognized him on the television broadcast?"

"Yes. One son was a social worker, the other a policeman," answered Opal.

"Their widowed father had been a very strict man with his sons when they were growing up. No quibbling about what was right or wrong, no shades of gray," said Agatha. "Yet one son wanted to turn his father into the police and the other didn't. They both knew that if their father was found guilty, he'd get the death penalty or go to prison for the rest of his life."

"Guess which son turned in their father?" Opal asked the kids.

"Policemen are good people," offered Justin.

"I vote with Justin. The cop gave up his father," said Luna. She didn't hold much fondness for the police. They always seemed to hover on the periphery of teenage gatherings on the Duxbury beaches.

"I think it was the social worker," said Sola. She had a greater appreciation for people in mental health services than did any of the others. "He wanted to do what was right."

"What would you do in the same situation?" Harriet was delighted that, for once, the family was holding a civil, intelligent conversation.

"I didn't kill anyone," whispered Sola.

Everyone ignored her remark.

"Rat out my Dad? Are you kidding? Now if it had been you, Mom, that's another story." Luna grinned.

"Thanks, darling. I appreciate your vote of confidence." Harriet turned to Justin. "What about you? What would you do if you saw your father on television committing a crime?"

"I'd come and tell you, Mommy." He reached over and grabbed a piece of French bread.

"Snitch," said Luna.

"Good boy," said Opal. "You're going to grow up to be a diplomat. You know which side of the bread is buttered."

"I'm going to be a policeman," he answered, while examining both sides of his slice of bread.

"Are we on target? Was it the cop?" asked Luna.

"He's crying," said Sola. "He told because he had to and now he's crying."

"She's right." Agatha nodded toward Sola. "It was the social worker, and his father won't forgive him. Says his son betrayed him."

"You mean the cop kept silent?" Luna shook her head in disbelief.

"His defense is that he wasn't absolutely sure it was their father in the video. But he knew. You can tell by the way he acted on the witness stand. Lying like a dog. Once close, the brothers are now enemies," said Agatha.

"He's crying outside. He's crying inside," added Sola.

"The social worker did the right thing, and now he's lost his whole family." Harriet sighed.

"And without family, who are you?" asked Opal.

Every weekend, Agatha disappeared, returning on Sunday night. No one dared probe into her trips, except for Opal late one night, getting ready for bed.

"Where do you go?" she asked.

"To ceremony, Grandmother. I go back to my people. I go back to the Spirits of this turtle continent, to thank Them for my life, to ask Them to help me live as a human being." Agatha sensed there was no hidden bias to the old woman's questions, no doubt, no disdain.

"What do these Spirits tell you?"

"They answer my questions. They tell of the future and what is needed now. Our medicine people travel through the dimensions. The Spirits talk to them, and then they come back and tell us what was said."

"Sounds like the ancient Greek mystery religions. People would come far and wide to ask questions of the Delphic Oracle, and she'd tell them what to do," said Opal. She pointed to a book on Greek mythology and history high up on the shelf. "You might read that one. People now look back and try to understand her appeal. There are a lot of things we human beings have forgotten over time."

"You're not a Christian then, Grandmother? I thought with the name of McCarthy, you'd be Catholic."

"I was raised Catholic, taught the importance of faith and obedience. But when I saw what foolishness the male priests had to say about women, babies, marriage, and things they simply couldn't understand, I stopped going to church. I started reading. Did you know that Jesus parachuted into old stories, myths that had been around centuries before he was ever born?"

Agatha shook her head.

"If you read about the old mystery religions, you'll discover the myths of the miraculous birth in the manger, the virgin mother, the crucifixion, and the resurrection existed long before Jesus ever came on the scene. The old stories are all there."

"So you don't believe that Jesus was a real person?"

Opal shrugged her thin shoulders. "I don't know, but the descriptions of what he said and what he did came many decades after his death. Stories of martyrs always evolve to fit the political and spiritual questions of a particular time and place."

Agatha pulled down the book and began to thumb through it.

"Do your medicine people do healing ceremonies?" asked Opal.

Agatha looked up from the book. "Yes. They ask the Spirits to come and work on the person needing help."

Opal hesitated, then asked, "Can they help Sola?"

"I don't know, Grandmother."

"Can you find out?"

"Perhaps, but I'll have to ask Harriet's permission first."

"You know, when I was younger, I used to dream of what it must have been like to be the Delphic Oracle. All that potential power to help others."

"And the burden of it," added Agatha "I'll read the book. Thank you, Grandmother."

Harriet had lots of questions she wanted answered first. "Who is this medicine person?"

"Eagle Wing Woman."

"What will she do with Sola?"

"I'm not sure," said Agatha, "Probably a Sacred Pipe ceremony."

"I don't want Sola drinking or swallowing any hallucinogenic drugs, mushrooms, or the like."

"No, we don't use any of that funny stuff. She'll be safe."

"Do you need money to pay the woman for this healing work?"

Agatha shook her head. "No, a medicine person can't charge for healing ceremonies. We'll bring the gift of tobacco."

It reflected both her sense of desperation and her trust in Agatha that Harriet was willing to agree to most anything. "Do you want me there?"

"I think it better that I take her alone with me. Less outside noise, interference." Agatha didn't want Harriet's natural skepticism to interfere with the healing process.

On Saturday morning, Agatha and Sola headed to the camp of Eagle Wing Woman. After a ninety-minute ride, Agatha's truck bumped down a long wooded road to the medicine woman's house.

"Is she really old like Grandma?" asked Sola.

Much to her surprise, Eagle Wing Woman turned out to be a robust, dark-haired, middle-aged woman, neither old nor young. Sola's hand reached out with the gift of tobacco. "This is for you," she said.

"Thank you, Sola," said the woman, taking Sola's hand and holding it, "for showing the ways of respect."

"My mind gets confused," said Sola.

"There are many voices in you," said the woman.

"Yes, they say mean things to me. Can you stop them from doing that?"

They talked some more. "Lie down on your back," she told Sola. She smudged the girl, using her eagle wing and the smoke of burning sage. Eagle Wing Woman then unwrapped her medicine bundle, assembled her Sacred Pipe, filled it, and prayed for Sola's health.

Sola closed her eyes.

Eagle Wing Woman blew some of the smoke from the Sacred Pipe over the girl. She prayed some more, then went deep into the silence. At first curious and scared, Sola watched the woman but when nothing hurtful happened, the girl relaxed, closed her eyes, and rested.

Eagle Wing Woman sang and talked to the Spirits, nodding her head when They spoke back to her. Agatha kept her eyes wide open but didn't see any Spirits.

At the end of the ceremony, the medicine woman blew out her Pipe and placed it back in the bundle. "You can get up now," she told Sola, but Sola had fallen asleep. "Let her sleep," said the medicine woman to Agatha. "We'll go into the other room and talk."

Tiptoeing into the kitchen, they sat down to drink strong coffee. Agatha was quiet, waiting for Eagle Wing Woman to share what she had learned from the Spirits.

"Life will be hard for this one," she began. "Things are messed up inside. She has a sister?"

"Yes," said Agatha.

"Better this one than that one. Spirits say that there is no healing here. Better to follow white man's medicine. Keep looking. Pay attention. Something about a lightning bug will show the way." She slapped her hands on her thighs. "That's all I can tell you."

"Okay," said Agatha. It was time to wake up Sola and go home.

Harriet was dancing with Justin and singing love songs when they returned to Duxbury. "How did it go?" she asked, as Justin left the room.

Agatha repeated what the medicine woman had said.

"Lightning bug, huh? I can't see how that would be of much help. Did she have fun?"

"Sola slept through most of the ceremony."

"That probably means I should reduce her medication. You know my mother sometimes comes up with the craziest ideas. She keeps looking for that Delphic Oracle. Thank you for taking Sola anyway."

"Sometimes it works, sometimes it doesn't," explained Agatha.

"It's okay. It's your way, not ours. No criticism intended." Harriet knew she had sounded dismissive of the medicine woman. "It's just that everywhere I look, I keep ending up in dead end alleys. Nobody knows how to help her."

Justin wandered back into the room, and the two women stopped talking. He held out his hand to Harriet. "C'mon, Mommy, show me how to do that dance."

Harriet rolled her eyes. "Could you possibly work Monday night? I won't get home until late."

"Sure. The bank works you hard."

"Oh no, that's not it," said Harriet raising her eyebrows. "I've got a dinner date."

NINE

Sola, Justin, and Opal had all long gone to bed, before Harriet arrived at the house with her Internet date. Luna kept looking out the living room window, disturbing Digger who was fast becoming her lapdog. "When is she going to come home?"

"The watched pot will boil in its own good time," said Agatha fully engrossed in watching the movie *Smoke Signals* for the fourteenth time. "Oh, I love this part, when the girls drive the car backwards." She clapped her hands with glee.

Luna flopped onto the couch. "Why do you keep looking at that stupid movie?"

"Because it makes me feel at home."

"Did you live on a reservation?"

"Yeah. I grew up surrounded by my aunties."

"You miss it?"

Agatha wagged her head back and forth. "Yes and no. Lot of poverty, unemployment. Things changed when they got a casino. At first, they wanted everybody to get on the rolls. Then when the casino came in, they started kicking everyone off the rolls."

"The rolls?"

"To be a member of a tribe, you have to be enrolled. For those tribes with state or federal recognition, they're pretty strict about who's a member and who isn't."

"You mean that blood quantum stuff?"

Agatha nodded. "It's all about money. Native Americans can be just as greedy as white people. I know one tribe that applied for a casino. A bunch of Anglo investors, big CEO people, offered to front them the money, but the tribal chairman read the contract that gave these white people twenty-five percent of all future tribal resources. He said 'hell no.' So the white CEO told him, 'You're now our enemy.' Then they snuck behind his back and slipped money to other candidates in the next tribal election. The tribal members voted out the guy with the smarts, put in a fellow with a high school education. The white people came back with an even worse contract, one that eventually gave them all the tribal land. Since the Council members didn't know squat about contracts, they signed away the tribe's sovereignty and birthright."

"Can they do that?"

"Past, present, and future. This country worships money, and it doesn't matter what color of skin you possess."

"I heard something, a car door." Luna jumped up from the couch, dumping Digger on the floor, and ran to the window.

Digger scrambled to his feet. Agatha turned off the television. "Quick, get the dog. He'll jump all over your mother's date."

Luna grabbed Digger by the collar and dragged him away from the door, hacking and coughing, front feet pawing the air.

The door opened. Harriet entered, followed by a distinguished-looking gentleman of moderate height, his white hair short, his mustache trim, his face kind. "It's a welcoming party," she said.

He tipped his head at Agatha, Luna, and the wiggling dog. "Digger, I presume?"

Luna let go. Digger rushed at Harriet, then thrust his nose into the man's crotch.

"This is Travis Steele. My daughter, Luna, and Agatha Stands. Digger, come here," said Harriet.

"Glad to meet you." He pushed the dog off and held out his hand.

Luna shook it. "Are you a musician? Your name sounds like a stage name."

He shook his head. "No, but I play the banjo."

Agatha stayed in the background, studying him. She figured that he was in his late sixties but in damn fine shape.

Harriet turned toward him. "I had a really nice time, Travis. You must be tired and ready to head home."

"Would you like a cup of coffee first?" interrupted Agatha. "Won't take but a second."

Harriet pivoted and shot Agatha a look of dismay, then smiled at Travis. "Really, we can't impose on you like this."

"I can make decaf, if you prefer," interjected Agatha.

"Don't mind if I do," replied Travis Steele.

"Well, I'm going to bed," announced Luna. "Nice to meet you, Mr. Steele."

Harriet found it difficult to keep her eyes open during the next thirty minutes of conversation, most of which had to do with different banjo picking styles. Finally she said, "I have to be up early for work tomorrow morning."

"Excuse me," Travis said, "I've been having such a good time with you lovely ladies, that I wasn't paying attention to the clock. When you're retired, time doesn't carry the same pressures. I must be going. Thank you, Harriet, for a wonderful evening." Before departing, he took her hand and kissed it, then picked up Agatha's hand and kissed it as well.

The two women cleaned up the kitchen, the cups, and the coffeepot.

"Whatever possessed you to invite him in for coffee, Agatha? He's a bit on the old side for me. Next time, I'll put down an upper age limit."

"Nice man, though," said Agatha stacking the dishwasher. "Got a good heart to him."

"Were there any problems tonight?" asked Harriet as she scrubbed the sink.

"Luna came into the bathroom when I was helping Grandmother with her bath. She asked, 'Grandma, have you ever had an extramarital affair?'"

Harriet put down the sponge. "Good grief. What did my mother say?"

"She fixed Luna with a beady eye and replied, 'That's none of your goddam business.'"

"Good for her," said Harriet. "She may have some dementia, but she's still here with us."

"I found Justin asleep in Sola's bed. Apparently Sola needed some company. I carried him into his own room."

"Sometimes she gets really scared at night. Of what I don't know. She'll bribe Justin to come stay with her."

Agatha noted the drag of sadness filter into Harriet's voice.

Harriet shook her head as if to clear her mind of such thoughts. "Well, I must be off to bed. Busy workday tomorrow."

"Will you be needing me to cover another night in the near future?" Agatha raised her eyebrows.

"I don't know if I'm really ready to get back out into the meat market. After Winston, I'm not sure I know how to do this man/woman thing anymore. I really loved him, but . . ." Harriet paused, not sure how much to share with Agatha.

Aware of the strong, forgiving pull of silence, Agatha waited.

Harriet leaned against the kitchen counters, arms folded as if hugging herself. "Justin was my insurance, my glue to keep us together when things began to crack apart. Winston thought Justin was a mistake. After Sola, he wasn't interested in having any more children. As Speaker of the House, he had taken a public, pro-life stance, but when it came to us, he suggested that I get a secret abortion."

"It's the way of politicians."

"But I wanted this gift of new life because I sensed, without knowing it, that our relationship was unraveling in all the little moments between us. There's a universe in those little spaces of time, isn't there?"

"The little stories mirror the larger story. We only see what's happening when we're ready. By then, it's usually too late," added Agatha.

"One love affair is enough," said Harriet. "I don't know if I have the stamina to endure another."

"Men can be difficult," said Agatha, "but I wouldn't give anything for all that learning."

"I read the newspaper this morning. He was found guilty of murder," Harriet announced at the dinner table the next night.

"Who?" asked Opal.

"The murder trial, Mom."

"What murder trial?"

"The one you and Agatha attended."

"Oh," Opal said. She'd already forgotten it. An image of the courtroom stirred in her brain, but the details remained foggy.

"So should he get the death penalty?" Harriet asked the kids, hoping to stir up another rousing table discussion.

"I don't believe in that eye for an eye stuff," said Luna.

"Me too," echoed Justin.

"I smell burning flesh," muttered Sola.

"The electric chair?" asked Luna.

Justin twisted in his seat, looking for wires.

"Agatha, what do you think?" asked Harriet.

Agatha shrugged her shoulders. She didn't much like capital punishment, thinking too many poor people end up on death row for the wrong reasons. But she knew there were some evil people in the world who didn't deserve to live among other human beings.

"Well," said Harriet, "I think this man deserves to die for killing that young store clerk."

Agatha shot her a glance. "I thought you were pro-life."

"When it comes to the young and the innocent, yes. I oppose abortion, but when it comes to murderers, I believe in capital punishment."

"Mom, that's not being pro-life," said Luna. "I can't stand it when you're so inconsistent. Why can't you be more like Dad?"

Harriet glanced over at Justin. "Thank God, I'm not."

Late at night, after everyone had gone to bed and fallen asleep, the police arrived in three squad cars and pounded on the front door.

Harriet stirred first to the thumping noise downstairs. Agatha woke to the flashing lights reflecting like a kaleidoscope on the ceiling. By the time Harriet reached the first floor, Agatha had paused at the head of the stairs.

Harriet unlocked the door.

Policemen stood there, guns drawn, vigilant and tense.

"What's the problem?" asked Harriet. "Is there a burglar outside?" She pulled her bathrobe tighter around the collar.

Agatha shrank back into the stairs' darkness.

"We got a call from here. Said there were dead bodies everywhere. We're going to have to do a search, Ma'am." The policeman moved into the foyer, followed by four other officers.

"That's ridiculous," protested Harriet, "Who called?"

"A girl. She was crying and scared. We have to check it out, room by room, Ma'am."

"Wait a minute. I think I know what happened. I have a mentally ill daughter. Please, put away your guns. You'll only scare my kids to death. Let me get her."

Harriet dashed up the stairs, past Agatha standing in the shadows.

"Where is Sola?" Before Agatha could answer, Harriet threw open the door to Sola's room. The girl crouched in a fetal position on the bed, eyes wide open.

"Sola, did you call the police?"

Sola didn't answer.

Again, Harriet asked, "Did you call the police?"

"There were dead people all around. I saw them, everywhere."

Harriet yanked Sola to her feet and threw a bathrobe on her. "Come with me."

"I'm scared of the stairs, Mommy."

"I'll help you," Harriet said, feeling irritated that Agatha had not come into the room to help.

Sola held tightly onto her mother's arm as they made slow progress down the stairs to the waiting policemen.

"Did you call them on the telephone?" Harriet asked.

Sola shyly glanced at the officers and nodded.

"What did you tell them?" Harriet persisted.

"There were dead people, everywhere."

"Okay, Sola, now show us these dead people," Harriet said.

"They're gone now."

"I think we get the picture, Ma'am." The officer tipped his hat. "Sorry to have disturbed you. We have no choice when we get calls like that but to follow through."

"The mind works in mysterious ways." Harriet glanced at her daughter, a look part-frustration, part-sympathy.

"Can I go back to bed?" asked Sola, as the policemen left.

"You can't do this to us, Sola. When you're scared, come into my room and wake me. If you make more calls like this, someone will come along and cart you off to a hospital."

"Mommy, you won't send me away, will you?"

"Promise not to call the police again?"

Sola nodded, but Harriet knew it was a promise that her daughter would have trouble keeping.

"I can't have Sola staying over at my place, if she's going to do things like that," said Winston.

"I need a break, Winston," said Harriet. "I'm tired."

"Look, I'm paying good money for her therapist and for that Stands woman to stay there. What more do you want?"

"It's not the money. It's the responsibility. I can never get away."

"Look, I didn't invite *my* mother to live with us. Nor did I think we ought to have other children after the twins. And as for the dog, I told you we should have taken him to the pound."

"Where they would have put him to sleep," asserted Harriet.

"I'll take Justin and Luna this weekend. That should help some. I'll pick them up after school." Winston hung up, not willing to negotiate any longer.

Soon after Agatha left for the weekend, Luna and Justin departed for the visitation with their dad. It snowed six inches on Saturday. Sola stayed in her room most of the day, crying or sleeping, while Opal watched television. When it came time to help Opal to bed, Harriet reminded her, "We need to brush your teeth." She squeezed out some toothpaste onto the brush and handed it to her mother.

"It's got arsenic in it." Opal pushed the toothbrush away.

"Did you watch an Agatha Christie movie? Okay, maybe it's not a good night to brush teeth." Harriet washed out the toothbrush and put it back into the cup. She then helped her mother into bed and pulled up the covers.

"Good night, darling." On Opal's face appeared a familiar, old smile.

Harriet sat down on the edge of the bed. "Do you ever miss Dad? I do. I used to feel safe around him. Life was simpler then."

Opal patted her on the hand and rubbed her thumb along Harriet's skin. A mother's gentle touch.

She's still here, thought Harriet. *Underneath all those synaptic tangles, she's still here.*

TEN

Justin was unnaturally quiet upon his return home on Sunday afternoon.

"How did it go?" Harriet greeted him with a big hug.

"Okay." He headed up the stairs, his backpack trailing dirty clothes.

Luna appeared next in the doorway. "Hi, Mom."

"What happened? Did your father's new girlfriend get angry at Justin?"

Luna sloughed off her winter jacket onto the foyer table. "Nah, Justin played video games most of the weekend. Do you mind if I go call Judy?"

"Both of you are being mighty tight-mouthed about something." Harriet could smell a rat a mile away.

"Justin and I just hung out a lot together in the bedroom. It was kind of boring."

"So you don't like this new girl?"

"Caitlin? No, she's really cool. I liked her a lot." Luna started heading up the stairs.

"What are you not telling me?" Harriet stood at the bottom of the stairs.

Luna turned around. "She and Dad got in a big fight. She was angry at him about something at work. He accused her of trying to control him. I made sure that Justin and I stayed well out of it."

"Good thinking, hon. So how did it end up?" Harriet was dying to know.

"Dad yelled at her. He said, 'I didn't leave one bossy woman to take up with another.' She packed up her stuff and left. I think she was crying."

For the first time, Harriet felt a shred of sympathy for the hapless Caitlin.

"Now, can I go talk to my friends?" asked Luna.

Controlling indeed, thought Harriet. *He should examine his own mirror. He deserves to be the one rejected.*

Agatha returned from her weekend of ceremony and friends. More and more, she needed the break from the McWhinnie household with all its pressing problems. The invasion by police unnerved her and made her think of quitting. But she had promised Harriet she wouldn't leave until things improved. Too many things left undone and dangling.

Every time, she walked with Opal, she leashed the reluctant Digger, forcing him to heel between the two of them. At first, she rewarded him with little treats for staying by Opal, then had Opal dole them out. Digger grew fat with all of Opal's indulgence. It made the old woman happy to have a dog by her side, someone to love and pet whenever she felt like it. "It's like being with Edgar," she said.

Agatha continued to drive Luna to the weeknight agility lessons. Digger proved to be a smart dog, if increasingly roly-poly. Time came for him to conquer the daunting eight foot A frame. Digger made a mad dash but could only get to the middle rungs before gravity took over. He turned around and retreated.

"Dog's got to lose weight," said the trainer.

"We'll go on a diet," promised Luna. The last time she had studied her own reflection, she had cast a jaundiced eyes upon her own developing curves. They didn't fit the image of the tiny boobs, butts, and boyish waists of fashion models.

"No more treats for you, kiddo," swore Luna. Digger bent his head in a soulful manner, sure that the girl had something for him to eat.

Winston purchased three notebooks for Sola and suggested that she keep a journal. "A therapist once told me that it helps to write down your feelings and thoughts."

Sola took the task to heart and wrote voluminously, finishing up the three notebooks in one week. She asked her mother to buy her some more. By the end of February, Sola had compiled a stack of notebooks. She didn't want anyone in the family to read them. "They're mine and they're secret."

Harriet thought it harmless enough.

One weekend day, Sola complained of feeling dizzy. "There's an ocean in my eye. My legs ache," she said.

"Why don't you go sit down in the living room?" suggested Harriet from the kitchen. A thump on the floor brought her running. Prostrate on the floor in massive convulsions, Sola had peed on herself. Harriet made sure that she didn't swallow her tongue and tried to keep her calm until the convulsive jerking ceased. She telephoned the doctor immediately, then Luna.

"Come home. I need to take your sister to the emergency room. I want you to stay with your grandmother and brother."

At the emergency room, the physicians concurred that Sola had suffered a grand mal seizure. "Has she ever had seizures before?"

"No."

"Has she ever demonstrated unusual behaviors?"

That question took almost thirty minutes to answer. Harriet described how her daughter slipped in and out of psychotic states, the way the medications would help for awhile and then no longer be effective. "None of it makes sense to me. And nobody seems to understand why she acts the way she does."

"Does she write a lot?"

"All the time," answered Harriet.

The doctors nodded as they conferred together. "We think she has an Epileptic Psychosis," they said. "If we can treat the underlying epilepsy, then maybe that will resolve the psychiatric symptoms. Meanwhile, we'll put her on a medication to prevent seizures."

"She's been on so many," said Harriet, afraid to believe, afraid to hope that, this time, maybe things could be different.

"Is she going to be all right?" Luna asked her mother upon their return.

"I hope so. Sola, you look beat. Why don't you go take a nap?"

"I'll help you with the stairs," said Luna, solicitous toward her twin.

Exhausted, Harriet picked up the kitchen telephone and dialed Winston's number. As it was ringing, she could hear the front door open to Digger's loud welcome. She checked her watch. *Must be Agatha.*

"Hello. Harriet?" A male voice issued from the foyer.

Oh God, she thought, *why does his voice still make my heart stop beating?* She hung up the phone, as his face appeared around the corner. He was holding something behind his back.

"Am I interrupting something?"

"No. In fact, I was calling you. To tell you about Sola."

Winston's hands emerged with a bouquet of daffodils. "Here. I thought you could use some cheering up. Luna called me and said you had to rush to the emergency room."

He knows that daffodils are my favorite flowers, the harbingers of Spring. "Thank you." Harriet took the bouquet and settled them into a vase.

"How is she doing?"

"She's upstairs, probably asleep by now. They said it was a grand mal seizure, that she has an Epileptic Psychosis."

"That's great. Now we've got a diagnosis that will explain what's going on with her. They have medications for that, don't they?"

Ever the pragmatist. There's nothing great about our daughter being psychotic, she thought. "They've put her on an anti-seizure medication."

"You've had a really tough time with her."

"So you've noticed?"

Winston sat down, brushed back his salt and pepper hair from that handsome face that he used so well. A face that suggested intelligence, confidence, and witty flirtatiousness. "Got any coffee?"

"The kids say you broke up with your girlfriend." Harriet couldn't resist the little jab. Back turned toward him, she retrieved a coffee cup from the cupboard.

"Snooks, we can do better by our kids than fighting."

It had been a long time since anyone had used that nickname for her. She poured him a cup of coffee, sat down, and, elbows on the table, cupped her chin in her hands. "Winston, what do you want?"

"A truce."

"A reconciliation?"

"A truce. A cease fire. I'll try to be a better father, spend more time with them, give you a break, and . . ."

"Yes?"

He stared into the coffee cup as if reading the grounds. "I don't know how to put it as to please you."

"I'm listening."

"Harriet, you're like a wild cat, all coiled up, claws out, ready to pounce on me."

The sound of the front door opening interrupted them. Agatha had returned. She entered the kitchen, stopped and looked at the two of them seated at the kitchen table.

Winston stood up and held out his hand. "I'm Mr. McWhinnie."

Agatha shook his hand. "I'm Miz Stands." She dropped his hand and turned toward Harriet. "You want me to leave you two alone?"

"Yes," said Winston.

"No need," answered Harriet.

Agatha slowly retrieved a cup from the cupboard and poured herself some coffee. "Just go on with your talking, like I'm not here."

"Harriet," he began, doing his best to ignore Agatha, "I'm about to introduce a new piece of important legislation, The Family Act, to help parents afford pharmaceutical resources for their children with emotional and behavioral disabilities."

"Go on," Harriet said.

"Well, it's not common knowledge that I have a mentally ill daughter."

"You've made sure of that, Winston, by keeping her out of sight when in the public."

He held up his hand. "Yes, I want to rectify that."

"How?"

Nervously he rubbed his forehead. "I want to bring Sola out into the light, let the public know her better. She'd be—"

"The poster child for your new Family Act?" interrupted Agatha.

A smile escaped onto Harriet's face.

"Well, I want to spend some quality time with her," he said.

"In front of the cameras?" suggested Harriet.

"Of course there will be some filming of her."

"Maybe you could even have her therapist talk to the public about her problems?" added Agatha.

"Not a bad idea. Do you think that's possible?" Winston looked at Harriet.

"Anything's possible," said Harriet. "Perhaps we can show how climbing stairs occasionally precipitates panic attacks?"

"Even better," said Agatha, "why don't we get her to talk about all the dead bodies she sees in the house?"

"I don't think the public is ready for that. Do you, Snooks?"
Again, Winston turned to consult with Harriet.

Underneath the table, Harriet was digging her fingernails
into the palm of her hand as the rage boiled up inside of her.
It was all she could do to restrain herself from jumping up and
beating him to the ground. *I don't believe in violence. I don't
believe in violence*, she silently recited.

"I think you better go, Mr. McWhinnie," cautioned Agatha.

"Excuse me," he said. "This is my house."

"No, it's not," Harriet said, "And you better leave while
you can."

Winston got up. "It's a good Act. Something that could
help Sola."

"Out," said Agatha, pointing the way.

A stormy look came over his eyes, a man rarely denied. Jaw
tensed, eyes set to steel, he brushed by Agatha, saying, "I don't
know who you are, but you're no friend of mine." He slammed
the front door behind him.

"Thank you," said Harriet. "I'm sorry that you got caught
in the middle."

"That's okay."

"No, it's not. He's a rather powerful man. He doesn't tend
to make frivolous threats toward those he considers to be
his enemy."

Agatha raised her eyebrows. "He called you Snooks."

"It's his special nickname for me. Recently, I looked up the
definition. Snook means to sniff or sneak around, a large,
vigorous sport fish, or a contemptuous thumbing of the nose.
Take your pick." She paused. "Things were simpler then, when
I didn't need to know the meaning of things."

Sola bloated up with the anti-seizure medication, while Luna shrank herself into smaller and smaller sizes. After a meal, Luna would automatically head to the bathroom and stick a finger down her throat. The retching left her throat sore, so she sucked on cough drops.

Only Opal seemed to notice the changes that started coming over Luna. "You got a tapeworm, girl?" she asked. "You're getting skinnier than a string bean."

Agatha attributed the loss of weight to Luna's agility workouts with Digger.

Harriet was too busy between her job and taking Sola to doctors' appointments to notice Luna's weight loss. *Thank heavens, there haven't been any more seizures*, she thought.

At times, a ravenous hunger would consume Luna, and then she couldn't stop herself from gorging on chocolate candy bars and salty corn chips. But no sooner had she satisfied herself with a thousand quick calories, she vomited it back up. Her energy levels dipped as her starving body ran out of sufficient blood sugar to sustain high activity.

She fainted in gym class. They sent her home with the diagnosis of "possible flu" but no fever ever developed.

"She's got tape worms, I tell you," Opal told Agatha. "They're sapping the energy right out of her."

But even Agatha was fooled by Luna's protestations.

"Everything is fine," the teenager said. "Just leave me alone. I'm fat enough as it is without everyone getting concerned with my appearance."

Agatha had great sympathies for the raging foolishness of adolescent hormones. For someone who had shown little interest in men for a long time, she felt quite unprepared for her sudden surge of interest in a particular gentleman.

A couple of telephone calls was all that it took to get her flustered, red-faced, and closed-mouth about it all.

"Miz Stands got a boyfriend," Sola announced one evening.

All eyes pivoted toward her around the dinner table.

"Is that why you've disappeared during some of the evening hours as of late?" Harriet passed the spaghetti bowl.

Agatha shrugged her shoulders.

Luna heaped three spoonfuls on her plate, then doused it with a river of tomato sauce. "I think she's embarrassed."

"It's none of your goddamn business," said Opal, picking up a strand of spaghetti with her finger and sucking it into her mouth. Justin imitated his grandmother's fingering of the food.

"Mom, watch your language," said Harriet, "and your table manners. Justin, use your fork."

"'Fess up. Who is it?" asked Luna, not to be deterred.

Agatha put down her utensils and dabbed her mouth with the napkin. "I can see there will be no peace for me tonight. You'll see for yourself." She consulted her watch. "He's picking me up in a few minutes."

Sure enough, barely had ten minutes flown by when there came a solid knocking on the front door.

It was a footrace between Justin, Luna, and Digger as to who was going to get there first. Agatha stood up, straightened her blouse, patted her hair, and gathered her pocketbook. Luna opened the door, and in stepped a distinguished-looking, white-haired man with a a trim mustache and a kind face.

"Hello Digger. Justin. Luna. Agatha. Hello Harriet."

Harriet rose from the table. "It's good to see you again, Travis. I hope you weren't upset by my letter."

"Oh no, I fully understood. You and I are of quite different generations. Well, Agatha, are you ready for an adventure?" Travis' eyes sparkled.

Agatha gathered her winter jacket and headed for the door. "I won't be back until quite late," she announced.

"Enjoy yourself. No need to hurry back." Harriet grinned.

"It's not that." Agatha blushed. "We're driving to a hospital where Travis volunteers. He plays the banjo for the patients there."

"Oh," said Harriet, feeling a little disappointed in her romantic expectations.

It was a long drive in the dark, moonless night. Travis lived west of Boston, whereas the McWhinnies resided south of the city.

"It's a big mental hospital, a teaching hospital for Harvard. Many famous people have been patients there." They headed up a long, luxurious drive into the campus of the private hospital.

Agatha whistled. "Looks to me like a place for rich people."

"Or those with good insurance," he added. He drove around to the back of a building, parked, and pulled out his banjo. "This is the Developmental Disabilities unit. Come on, you can carry the sheets of music for the sing-along."

As they walked toward the lit building, Agatha noticed a chunky black woman in her mid-thirties striding ahead of them. There was nothing particularly striking about the woman, except for a tiny light blinking off and on, off and on, over her left shoulder.

"What's that?" asked Agatha.

"What?" Travis' eyes followed her pointing finger.

"Over that woman's shoulder."

"Looks like a firefly. Can't be. Not the right season for it." Travis shook his head.

The light flickered around the back of the woman's head.

"But that's what it is," said Agatha in a hushed voice. "It's a lightning bug." Agatha thrust the sheets of music into Travis' free hand and took off running toward the woman.

"Excuse me, excuse me." She caught up to the woman and touched her elbow. "I need to talk to you."

"Yes? And you are?"

"Agatha Stands. Do you work here?"

The woman nodded. "I'm Dr. Sherman, the neurologist for the Disabilities Unit."

"Just the person I need to talk to." Agatha watched the lightning bug blinked four times, then disappear.

"I've got an appointment in five minutes."

"Then I'll be real brief. I take care of a teenager, a twin, with lots of things wrong with her. She's fifteen, born with one kidney, cleft palate, cerebral palsy, and lots of learning disabilities. But she's not retarded, just in her own world at times. The doctors say she's psychotic."

"And her twin? Are they identical? Do they have the same problems?"

"No, they're quite different from each other."

"What about medication? Has that worked with her?"

Travis caught up to them.

Agatha shook her head. "Her mother says they work for a time then stop being effective. Nobody really knows what's wrong with her."

"Who's in charge of her treatment?"

"Her psychiatrist and therapist."

Dr. Sherman started walking toward the Unit again. "It's cold out here. Look, I don't want to interfere, but I suspect that she has a genetic disorder. She needs to be seen by a pediatric neurologist, not an adult neurologist. They're generally not as keen on the chromosomal problems. I can give you some referral names, if you would like."

"Yes," said Agatha. *Thank you, little lightning bug*, she silently prayed.

That night, Agatha returned home after a delightful evening of off-key singing, joyful banjo music, a list of pediatric neurologists, and an unexpected but prolonged kiss from Travis Steele on the McWhinnie porch. Caught off-guard by his romantic gesture, Agatha didn't even notice the dark automobile idling across the street. Inside the car, the driver lowered the window, raised his camera, adjusted the telephoto lens, and clicked away.

ELEVEN

"C'mon, time to go to agility class." Agatha gently shook Luna who had fallen asleep over a school book.

"I'm too tired. You go," she protested.

"Digger's not my dog. He's yours. C'mon."

"He's Dad's dog." Luna sat up on the bed, groaned, and tried to collect herself. "Or was once."

"Not anymore. Digger looks to you as the alpha bitch."

"Thanks. Like I needed to know that." Luna pushed herself to her feet and gathered her jacket.

In the car, Luna yawned herself awake. "Is it okay if I ask you something?"

"Sure."

"If you knew someone really well and that person was doing something wrong, would you tell the police?"

Agatha shrugged her shoulders. "Depends who the person was and what they were doing. For example, if I had a friend that was taking drugs that would kill them, sure I'd tell someone. Probably their parent or spouse. I'd want to save a life."

"What if it was a family member?"

"Probably even more so. But I don't think this is about drugs, is it? Justin's too young, Sola's already medicated, and your grandmother prefers alcohol. Are you worried about your Mom?"

Luna shook her head. "It's nothing really."

Agatha made a mental note to observe Harriet's behavior for the next few days. She could well understand Harriet needing to escape into drugs, but somehow that seemed out of character for her employer.

At the facility, the dog trainer had set up a long agility course requiring both canines and humans to run the distance. Luna fell halfway through and limped back to the chairs, dragging a protesting Digger. "I'm too pooped to do anymore. Let's go home."

In the intense light of the training center, Agatha noticed dark circles pouching under Luna's eyes. They drove home in silence for the first few moments, until Agatha pulled over and parked on a side street.

"Are you going to tell me what's going on with you?"

"I'm just tired, that's all," said Luna.

"I watched you running with him on the course. You're getting rail thin. You've lost that spark. So don't give me any bullshit. What's going on? Are you sick?"

Luna blushed, embarrassed by the unwanted attention.

"Are you taking drugs?" Agatha persisted.

"No, I'm not that stupid."

"Then don't lie to me. I don't respect people who can't tell the truth of themselves."

"A lot of people lie," said Luna, her voice tentative, hinting. "Not just kids. Adults too."

Agatha turned toward her. "I don't lie to you, Luna. Never have. I tell you like it is, and I expect the same back from you."

"There's a lot of things you haven't told us."

"That's different from lying. It's called discretion. When there's something you need to know, I'll tell you. Now, what's going on with you?" Agatha's dark eyes bore into Luna.

The girl turned away her face, answering in a small voice. "I puke a lot."

"I don't understand. Do you have an ulcer?"

Luna sighed with exasperation. "No. After I eat, I make myself sick. I stick a finger down my throat."

"Why would you do that?" *People are starving, and this rich kid throws up her wonderful meals,* thought Agatha. *Sometimes this world is bat shit crazy.*

"Because I'm fat. I don't care what others say. It's *my* body." Luna stuck out a defiant chin.

"Look at what you're doing to it. You've lost muscle tone. You're tired all the time. You complain that you're having trouble concentrating in school. Sounds to me like your body's shutting down. Hey, I don't care whether you are teensy weensy or chubby wubby, Luna, but you've got to keep your body strong and healthy."

"I am strong," she protested.

"Tell that to Digger then. He was the one putting out all the effort tonight, because he loves you. There's no excuse these days for a woman to go weak and wobbly. You want to be the equal to any man? Then you've got to be strong in your self and that self starts first with the body. You want to become a fragile creature, someone whom others can walk all over?"

The girl shook her head.

"I didn't think so. You keep on losing weight, you'll evolve into a flimsy little thing, someone with no gumption, no backbone, no way to kick ass. I'm telling you that the world out there is not a sweet, loving place that's going to be kind to you. You've got to be able to fight your own battles."

"Are you going to tell Mom?"

Agatha studied her. "Are you going to do something about it?"

"Like not throw up?"

"Restraint isn't enough, Luna. I want you to build some muscle. Do some weight lifting. Your father left some hand weights downstairs in the basement."

"I hate exercise."

"I'll work alongside you."

"What will you give me if I do that?" asked Luna.

"A healthy body. A strong body. Maybe someday, you'll even beat me in arm wrestling."

"If I beat you in arm wrestling, can I call you Agatha?"

"Even better. When that day comes, I'll tell you my full name." Agatha reached out and shook hands with Luna, a deal struck between them.

Opal's problems that week occurred at the other end. By holding everything in, she had become dreadfully constipated. The physician handed Agatha a bottle of phosophosoda.

"Have her drink this."

Opal refused. She clammed up her mouth, sucked in her lips, and shook her head. No amount of cajoling, bribery, or authoritative commands did the trick. Her belly swelled up. She looked like an octogenarian about to give birth to triplets.

"Mom, you have to swallow this medication. Or you're going to burst up and blow. One big swallow will do it." Harriet held the offending cup to Opal's tightly clenched mouth. "C'mon, you can do it."

Opal coughed and, in that brief opening, Harriet poured the medication into her mother's mouth.

Opal's eyelids squinched into mean, little slits. Cheeks pouched with the liquid, she surveyed the room and spat upon the cherished Oriental rug. "Don't ever do that again," she commanded in her Mother-As-Supreme-Commander voice.

Harriet dropped to her knees to wipe up the damage.

Agatha yelled, "Digger. Here boy."

The canine garbage collector arrived and promptly cleaned up the mess.

Angry, Harriet stood up and turned toward Agatha. "I can't deal with this right now. Take her back to the doctor tomorrow."

"You need an enema," said the physician the next morning.

"No," said Opal.

The physician handed Agatha the enema kit and spoke to Opal. "It'll make you feel a lot better."

"No," repeated Opal in a low, resolute tone of voice.

Agatha looked at Opal and then at the doctor, sizing up the situation. She thrust the kit back into his hands. "You do it."

"It's very easy," protested the physician.

"Good," said Agatha. "You do it then."

He sighed, bothered by the intransigence of elderly patients and the lack of initiative of some middle-aged women. He told the nurse to give Mrs. Opal McCarthy a ten milligram Valium. After thirty minutes of that happy, little pill in her bloodstream, Opal didn't give a hoot about anything.

They discovered that Opal was impacted. "No wonder she refused to drink the phosophosoda." After removing the cork, the physician flushed her colon.

"Feel better?" asked Agatha on the way home.

Opal responded with an angelic, Valium-induced smile.

"Life imprisonment," announced Harriet that night at the family dinner table, having just glanced at the day's newspaper.

"For me, Mom?" asked Sola.

"No, darling. For that father who was turned in by one of his sons." Harriet reached over and patted her daughter's hand.

"What about the death penalty?" asked Luna. "He killed a man."

"Apparently, there's no death penalty in Massachusetts," answered Harriet, "but I doubt he'll ever get out of prison."

"Or back with his family," said Luna. "What's happened to the two sons?"

"The father cut off all contact with the son who identified him," answered Harriet.

"I'm glad he's in jail. He was a bad man," added Justin.

"I feel sorry for the snitch," said Luna. "To be banished like that."

"Blood's thicker than water," offered Opal. "Without family, what are we?"

"Alone," answered Sola.

"I've got a girlfriend at kindergarten," announced Justin.

"Oh?"

"And nobody's gonna take her away from me." He stuck out his chest.

"Oh?"

"Because she's the ugliest girl in my class," he continued.

"I wish . . ." said Sola.

"Yes, darling," prompted Harriet.

"That I had a boyfriend."

"Maybe Mom can find you one on her next internet date," suggested Luna. "Like she did for Miz Stands whom we hardly ever see anymore at night." Luna glanced at Agatha's empty chair.

"Has it ever occurred to you that maybe she needs some time away from us?" asked Harriet.

"Do you think she's fallen in love?" asked Luna.

"That's none of your business, young lady," said Opal.

"I've never had one," continued Sola, trying to get a word in edgewise.

Oh Sola, you make my heart break. Things will never come easily for you, thought Harriet. *I won't promise you something that may never happen.*

"I love you," interjected Justin.

"You're her brother. You can't be her boyfriend." Luna turned toward Sola. "I don't have anyone special either."

"But you've had them in the past," said Sola.

Harriet's eyebrows raised.

"So what?" Luna didn't look at her mother. "It's not going to kill you to be without a boyfriend, Sola."

"There's no death penalty in Massachusetts," said Opal with a smile. "Just—"

"Life imprisonment," answered Sola.

It took Harriet a long time to arrange her work schedule and secure an appointment with a pediatric neurologist. The bank wasn't happy that Harriet McWhinnie had so many family emergencies consuming her attention. But they valued her expertise and connection to the Speaker of the House. She knew that she walked a tightrope among her many commitments.

When Winston tried to involve his daughter in the public promotion of The Family Act, Sola receded into the shadows, scared by all the jostling cameras and journalists. He didn't think it safe to let her be interviewed, because he couldn't predict what she might say. But the few shots of her, somewhat disheveled, sorrowful in expression, unbalanced in features were enough to evoke great sympathy for him and support for his legislation.

"My Princess," he called her.

That warmed Sola's heart, even though it had been a term previously reserved for her twin sister. She looked into her bedroom mirror, studying herself, and whispering over and over, "My Princess."

After a long day, Winston shucked his shoes and sat down on his leather coach before the blazing gas fireplace, whiskey glass in hand. Pleased that his new legislation was garnering support on the Hill, he let the tensions of the day unwind to the sounds of John Rutter's Requiem.

Regretting his earlier show of temper, he missed the cheerful chatter of Caitlin. She had been a contrasting tonic to the sobriety and dutifulness of Harriet. While he could appreciate the steady calm and maternal instincts of his former wife, a man sometimes needed someone who was willing to play and have fun. He liked strong women, bright women who challenged him.

Caitlin had not only left his bed but also her staff position in his office. Although she claimed that she was leaving for graduate school, he knew that she would have stayed on the job if only . . .

Winston waved his hand in front of his face. *If Onlys never brought anything but regrets. I'm a man who looks forward. Never backwards.* He got up and poured himself another double. It was pleasant to get slightly drunk in the privacy of his own apartment.

The phone rang. He heaved himself off the coach, a bit on the tipsy side, and picked up the receiver. "Yes?"

"Sam Spade here." The man chuckled at his own joke.

"What did you find?"

"There's nobody by the name of Agatha Stands. That's an alias."

"She's dark. Maybe an illegal immigrant. Wouldn't that be a shame?" Winston drained the glass. "I'd hate to think my wife, my ex-wife, was in violation of the law."

"I can dig further, find out who owns that truck of hers. It's got South Dakota license plates. But if she's smart, it's registered under someone else's name."

"Good. Do that. Anything else for me?" He could hear the rustle of paper.

"Yes. She's got a male friend, a Travis Steele."

"Anything on him?"

"You wanna stay away from him."

"Why?"

"I was working a case once, and he ripped me up one side and down the other."

"A cop?"

"No, a judge."

"Even worse," said Winston. "Tread softly, my man. Don't call me at work."

The line clicked in disconnect.

Winston deposited the glass in the kitchen sink. As he looked out the night window to the twinkling lights of the city, his reflection, etched in darkness, glared back at him.

TWELVE

The rain pelted down, scouring the wintry patches
of snow, revealing a mix of sodden, mud-brown earth, depleted
yellow straw, and an occasional, surprising patch of green. A
time of season when the wind wobbles from cold to warm and
back to cold again, a time when nothing is predictable, when
people grow tired of frozen landscapes and yearn for their own
rebirth. Being New Englanders, they knew that wish and hope
alone couldn't release the clenched jaws of a bitter winter.

Into the downpour, Harriet launched herself back out onto
the dating scene. With trepidation, she had signed up for a speed
dating party of professionals at a Boston restaurant, where
everyone wore ID tags containing a first name and number.

"You have eight minutes per date in which to ask each other
questions," announced the organizer. "At the sound of the bell,
the men must move on to another table. Women, you stay at
your assigned table. You're not to ask where each other lives,

what your date does for a living, or for telephone numbers. You all have score cards to indicate whether you would like to see this person again. We will collate that information afterwards and if both of you are interested in seeing each other, we'll provide the contact information. Is that understood? The bell will sound seven times for seven dates."

Harriet sat at a corner table. Self-consciously, she brushed back her hair. *What am I doing here? Winston would say the shrew was getting desperate.*

The bell rang.

A long-haired fellow, tall and skinny, appeared at her table. "Hi, I'm Albert and you're Harriet," he said bending over for a better view of her name tag and ample breasts.

As he sat down, she started to offer her hand but could see that he wasn't going to reciprocate. She quickly withdrew her hand.

"I wanted to come right over to your table when I saw you."

Harriet felt a warm glow surging through her. Maybe this evening wasn't going to be so bad after all.

"Because I like older women," he added.

It went downhill after that. She hadn't ever heard of any of his favorite bands. When she mentioned Gustav Mahler, he asked if that was a German rap artist.

Ding, the bell rang.

Albert disappeared, and Bruno materialized. Not only did the carefully coiffed, handsome man take her proffered hand, he kissed it with flair. It was enough to make Harriet blush.

"You have a beautiful, clear complexion," he said in a heavily accented voice. "And the curves of a sensual woman."

Harriet shifted in the chair. "Thank you. May I ask you what you do for fun?"

"Is it not obvious? I love women. If I were born a woman, I'd have become a lesbian. And good wine. You do know your wines, don't you?"

"White with fish, red with meat, champagne on New Year's Eve." For Harriet, humor and flirtation always went hand in hand.

"Do you like your wine dry?"

"Wet," she answered. "Wet and cold."

"No, please not the red. The red must always remain at room temperature. Never cold."

"I like whiskey," she continued.

"Ugh." He looked at her now with barely disguised disdain. "It has no subtlety on the palette. Nothing to be discovered there."

"But it has fire on the inside."

He shook his head and consulted his watch. Five long minutes to go.

The flare-up of her fire sputtered and died.

Ding, the bell finally rang.

Next a short man, Jacob, sat down and stole a glance at his crib sheet. "Harriet, how many long-term relationships have you had in the past?"

"Let me think." She counted on her fingers. "Three."

"Tell me about them. How did they each end?"

"One was with a boy in college. We dated for four years, then broke up because he wanted me to join his church. But in all faith, I couldn't."

"Because?"

"I'm not a Christian."

"You're Jewish then?" Jacob asked, excitement rising in his voice. "I'm also Jewish."

Harriet shook her head. "No, I'm not Jewish."

He sat back. "What about after college? Did you have any significant relationships then?"

"My husband. We were married for thirteen years, but it didn't work out between the pressures of his work, my work, and the children."

"Children?" His eyebrows shot up in alarm.

"Three of them," she answered.

"What about the other long-term relationship?"

"The other?"

"Yes. You mentioned three such relationships."

"My very first one was with my best friend Todd. We were inseparable. Early on, we vowed to marry each other." Harriet heaved a sigh.

"What happened?"

"He left me."

"There must have been a reason," Jacob pressed, trying to sniff out trouble.

Harriet leaned forward in a confessional whisper. "He was seven. I was six. His parents moved away. I don't know if I have ever recovered from that loss."

Jacob sat back. "I don't want you to think badly of me, but three children is a lot."

The understatement of the year, she thought. "I won't hold it against you."

She couldn't think of a single question to ask him.

And so it went, her scorecard empty, her responses bordering on double meanings until it came to the seventh bell. A man with a big Scottish/Irish face appeared at her table. Of burly chest and muscular build, he pulled out the chair and sat down. "My name is Thomas, but friends call me Tom. Glad to meet you, Harriet." He offered her a beefy hand.

He looks like a stevedore, she thought. *I wonder if there are any smarts sitting inside that big head with the bushy eyebrows?*

"The rain has me brain addled. So, why don't you ask your questions first." His smile was either merry or mischievous.

Harriet prided herself on being able to read people by their first appearance, but there was something about him that rattled her. *What do I have to lose by challenging him with the truth?*

"How do you feel about children? I have three of them at home," she said.

"That's quite a brood," he answered, "But you seem to have maintained your sanity. Or is that just an illusion?"

Harriet laughed and pressed onward, "I've got twin girls, both teenagers." *There, that should stir terror in him.*

"Are they as pretty as their mother?"

"One is mentally ill."

"Must break your heart. I know what it's like when you want people to be one way and they go the other direction."

Harriet looked into his eyes. *Nothing false there. Is he for real?* "My mother lives with us as well. Dementia."

"Good grief, you've a lot on your shoulders, Harriet. Is there no one to help you?"

"Yes, there's a woman who lives on the third floor, Agatha. She's a big help to me. I don't know what I'd do without her."

"And what about the children's father?" He paused. "Or is that a tender area on which I'm treading?"

Harriet squelched an observation about men not understanding that parental responsibilities should go beyond providing the basic necessities. *Maybe this man is different.* "Do you have any children?" she asked.

"I was married once. We tried but she didn't get pregnant. It could have been my fault. She wasn't willing for us to get it all checked out. You're lucky to have children."

"Sometimes," said Harriet, "I want to run away. It gets pretty chaotic at home."

"I bet."

"Other times, I just pull in, turn a deaf ear, call for Agatha. You can only deal with so much, you know?" She couldn't believe that in the space of a few minutes with a stranger, she had plunged into such an honest confession. "What about you? I've been the one doing all the talking, jabbering away."

"Maybe that's because what you have to say is more interesting. I have one last question."

"Yes?" Harriet steeled herself for the coup de gras, the question and answer that would turn this man away.

"Do you have a dog?" he asked.

"Yes, I do. Is that important?"

"Because I'm crazy about dogs. Where I'm living right now, I can't keep a dog."

Ding, the bell rang.

Harriet memorized Tom's number, wrote it down on her scorecard. *Digger, have I got someone for you!*

"This is My Princess," declared Winston at the news conference, drawing Sola from the back to the front of the podium. "She's the reason, the motivation, the inspiration for The Family Act."

Light bulbs flashed and blinded her. She put up her hand to shield her eyes, amazed and flattered that people were showing interest in her. Her father continued to speak into the microphone about the benefits of this particular piece of legislation. It was all blah blah blah to her.

The inside voices scrambled. *You're a bad person*, they said. *People don't really like you. They think you smell. They think you're really a boy. They're going to hurt you.* She edged away from the stage to get her distance. She put hands to her ears, trying to shut them out, but the voices only got louder.

Her father grew more and more impassioned with his words and political press. He didn't notice Sola moving off stage.

In the back of the room stood Caitlin, listening to Winston do what he did so well—grandstand in front of a receptive audience. She noted Sola's obvious distress and would have intervened, but it would not have been welcomed by Winston. There were things still left unsaid between them, feelings of anger and regret. It wasn't love that had deserted her with regard to him; it was respect. He had forgotten that the people, not the lobbyists, were his constituents, that service, not power, constituted the political contract.

She watched Sola slip off into the crowd, followed by a female journalist carrying a microphone.

"Excuse me," said the journalist catching up to Sola, her camera man right behind her. "I bet you're real proud of your father there."

Sola nodded but kept on walking.

The journalist trotted to keep up with her, then tagged her arm and thrust a microphone in her face. "What does the Family Act mean to you?"

Sola flinched at the physical contact and tried unsuccessfully to pull away. A low moan issued from the back of her throat. The inside voices screamed at her.

"What are you saying?" asked the journalist, unable to decipher the muttering.

"I didn't appreciate . . . raping me last night," she said. "Choking me by the throat."

"Who? Who?" asked the journalist.

Sola looked wildly around the crowd, saw her father, and pointed. "Him."

"Your father raped and choked you?" asked the journalist.

Sola yanked her arm clear and hobbled off toward the nearby park.

The journalist spun around to her camera man, asking. "Did you get that? Sensational!"

The journalist approached Winston after the speech and recounted Sola's words. "Would you care to comment on her accusations?"

"This is what I'm talking about and why we need this legislation," Winston answered. "People who are mentally ill will often say or do crazy things because they live in their own world. They need our help, our compassion, not exploitation by the press. If you run with this story, we'll sue you pure and simple. Now you must excuse me while I try to find my daughter."

He sent a staff member to track her down, but Caitlin had gotten there first. She discovered Sola crouching and hyperventilating in the public restrooms.

"You're going to be okay," she said to Sola.

"No, I'm not," the girl answered.

Caitlin guided her to a nearby deli, sat her down, and bought her a soda. That was where Winston's staffer found them. "Hey, Caitlin, how are you doing? Sola, your Dad wants to talk to you."

Sola looked scared.

"I'll come too," said Caitlin, taking Sola by the hand.

Upon arrival, they had to wait until Winston's inner office cleared of supporters.

"What are you doing here?" Winston grumbled at Caitlin. "I want to see my daughter, alone."

Wide-eyed, Sola looked around the room for something to lean on. "Wait for me," she begged.

Caitlin nodded.

Once inside his office, Winston turned toward his daughter, trying to restrain his anger. "What did you think you were doing out there when you accused me, your father, of raping you? What in the hell were you thinking? I'm trying to help you and this is the thanks I get? Jesus Christ!" His voice rose higher and higher.

"Daddy, please." Sola sank to her knees on his office carpet, hands pressed to her ears.

"For God's sake, get up, Sola," he demanded.

"I can't. I can't stand up." She began hitting her head with her fists.

"Stop it. Stop it right now," he ordered. He grabbed her wrists.

She pulled away from him, scrabbling on the floor. She scrambled under his desk, whimpering like a wounded animal.

"No, you don't," he said, his voice shaking with rage. He reached down and pulled her out, hoisting her to her feet.

She struggled to get away.

Hands on her shoulders, he shook her. "For Chrissake, Sola, shut up."

Caitlin burst into the room.

"Get out," yelled Winston, his jaw set, his eyes afire. He loosened his grip on his daughter.

Sola wrenched herself free and threw herself upon Caitlin. "I'm so scared," she whispered.

"I think it's time to go home." Caitlin wiped Sola's sweaty brow. "Just let yourself breathe, slowly. That's right." She put her arm around Sola and guided the trembling girl out of the room.

Caitlin called the McWhinnie household to get directions, arriving with Sola at the same time as did Harriet.

"Oh, there's going to be trouble," said Luna looking out the front window. "Mother and the mistress are about to meet. Why is Sola with her?"

"Let me see," said Opal, elbowing her way to a better view. "Agatha, come quick."

Down on the floor, Agatha was playing Candyland with Justin. "Are you kidding? I'm about to land on the Neopolitan ice cream."

"Is Mommy home?" asked Justin, looking up.

Agatha rose to her feet. As Luna started toward the front door, Agatha gently touched her on the arm. "Better that we leave things between them."

Caitlin with Sola approached Harriet to explain what had happen. Neither she nor Harriet were aware of the curious audience peering out the front window.

Sola, however, saw them and headed for the house. The front door flew open. Sola slammed the door behind her.

"Why did Caitlin bring you home?" asked Luna.

"Daddy blew up. Caitlin bought me a soda. She was kind to me. Will you help me up the stairs? I'm feeling kind of shaky."

Agatha offered her arm for support. As they arrived at the top of the stairs, Sola whispered, "He grabbed me and shook me hard. I didn't want Justin to hear about it."

"Are you hurt?"

Sola shook her head. "Scared, tired. I want to take a nap. I think Daddy forgot."

"What did he forget, Sola?" *That you're fragile, that you have inner voices you can't control, that you live in a different world from the rest of us?* Agatha tried not to show her anger.

"I think," she said. "I think Daddy forgot that I am his princess."

"That son of a bitch," exclaimed Harriet, storming through the front door. "I wish I could take him to court and have all visitations denied."

"Mom," warned Luna. "Justin has big ears."

"Can you believe it? He showcased Sola at a press conference for his Family Act. Is this the special time he promised they'd have together?"

"He means well, darling," said Opal. "Winston sometimes doesn't have the best judgement. You provided a good balance to him. It's a shame you two—"

"Mother, don't even go there. Where's Sola? I must talk to her, see how she's doing. The poor kid must have been traumatized by all this." Harriet charged up the stairs, as Agatha started down.

"Is she okay?"

Agatha nodded. "She's taking a nap, but you know Sola. She loves getting your hugs."

"I swear, Agatha, I'm going to kill that man before it's all over."

"You and me both," Agatha muttered.

"I think Mom likes Caitlin," said Luna, trying to stir up things as a way to gain information from Agatha. "Boy, she was madder than a wet hen at Dad. Is Sola, okay?"

"Is Daddy okay?" interrupted Justin. He understood that something had gone very wrong.

"Mom wants to murder him," answered Luna.

"A figure of speech only," Opal explained to Justin. "Your mother has a temper on her. Your Dad will be just fine."

"Come back to the game," said Agatha. "Otherwise, I'm going to win all by myself."

Justin trundled back to Candyland, but the images of all the colored gumdrops on the game board did nothing to ease his anxiety. "Is Caitlin going to live here?" he asked.

"Ha. Now wouldn't that be something? Mistress of the House," exclaimed Luna.

"Hush, Luna. She seems like a nice girl," said Opal.

"And she did rescue Sola. Don't forget that," added Agatha. "I'm sure Caitlin has her own home."

Agatha spun the wheel and moved her piece to the finish line. She clapped her hands. "I won."

Justin puckered up his mouth. "When I play with Daddy, he lets me win."

"If you always win in life, Justin, you'll never learn a darn thing." Agatha folded up the game board.

"But I like to win," he persisted.

"Your big sister to the rescue. I'll do it for you," announced Luna.

"You want to play Candyland?" asked Agatha.

"Nope, I've been lifting weights. Time to show you that I've got youth and strength on my side. Watch me, Justin." Luna placed her elbow on the table, hand up. "Do you dare, Miz Stands? I'm willing to fight for my brother's honor."

"You're crazy," said Opal.

Agatha replaced the board game on the shelf, then wiped the dust off her hands. She sat down, catacorner to Luna, bracing her elbow on the table and flexing her fingers. "If you win, you can call me Agatha. If I win, you have to play with your little brother for an hour this evening—whatever he wants to do."

Luna balked. If she lost, it would be a mind-numbing hour to sit with a five-year-old. She loved Justin but only in fifteen minute dosages. Yet she had confidence. Not only had she put on weight, but her biceps had grown stronger, firmer. It should be a breeze to topple someone in her late fifties. "Okay, you're on."

Opal and Justin gathered around the table. Harriet appeared downstairs in time to see the set-up. "I'm rooting for you," she whispered into Agatha's ear. "We adults have got to stick together."

Luna and Agatha placed their right hands together, palm to palm. "On your mark," said Harriet. "Get set. Go."

The two hands clenched. Luna gritted her teeth and squinched her eyes shut. The arms trembled. Luna pushed and pressed, but Agatha's hand didn't budge. The teenager opened her eyes and saw the middle-aged woman smiling, her face revealing no apparent strain. It was as if she was toying with Luna, letting the girl exhaust herself first.

Luna grunted and threw everything into one last effort, but nothing happened. Then slowly, surely Agatha guided Luna's hand down to the table top.

"I win," Agatha said in the same voice that she had used earlier with Justin.

"You win," echoed Luna. "But next time . . . ."

Agatha turned toward Justin. "See? She's got the right spirit. If you lose, always look to the next time."

Later that night, Travis slowly drove Agatha home from a dinner he had specially prepared for her: poached salmon, spinach salad, and sweet potatoes. She had only picked at her food. "Something's not right, Agatha," Travis said. "You've been real quiet tonight. Was my cooking that bad? Or have I said or done anything that offended you?"

"I'm a private person, Travis. I told you that the first time we went out."

"I don't mean to interfere, but something is worrying you. Can I help?"

Agatha wondered whether to take him into her confidence. Her life was her own responsibility. If she made a mess of things, then it was up to her to clean up the mess. But sometimes when you try to take care of your own problems, other people get hurt. They think you don't care about them.

Hesitating, she finally confessed. "Back on the reservation, somebody's been asking a lot of questions about who owns my truck."

"Isn't it registered under your name?"

"Yes and no." Agatha could see that Travis was confused by that answer. "There's a lot of trading that goes on among relatives on a reservation. You do me a favor. I do you a favor. My cousin got this truck from someone else and gave it to another cousin who then gave it to me. I pay for the insurance, but I send the money to them. That's why it doesn't have Mass. license plates. Do you understand?"

Travis wondered how many state laws were being violated by this arrangement, but that was beside his immediate concern. "Why is someone wanting information on you, Agatha? Are you in trouble?"

"I don't know," she answered. She turned to look out the car window as the world in darkness streamed past.

"I don't know," she whispered.

THIRTEEN

The next evening, Harriet drove straight from work to Winston's office, prepared for a showdown. Caitlin had provided her with all the ammunition she needed. Agatha had agreed to work late and prepare supper for the family.

Until his secretary announced her arrival, Winston didn't have the slightest idea that Harriet was coming. He rose from his desk, told his secretary to take an early leave. *Things might get a bit loud and nasty*, he thought.

"Yes, Harriet. What can I do for you?" He closed the door to outside ears.

"I'm not one of your constituents."

"Of course not. I presume, however, that this is not a friendly visit for old times' sake."

She sat down in a chair facing him. She said nothing. *All the better to make him sweat.* She wanted to hurt him for what he had done to Sola, to Caitlin, to her. Her mother didn't believe in acts of revenge, thinking it only cheapened the doer. But then again, her father had never hurt her mother with such indifference and neglect.

"I had nothing to do with that journalist," he said.

"I hate you." *Can he hear that?*

"Look, I know this is about Sola."

"You don't deserve her. All she's ever offered you is her unqualified affection. You exploited her."

"First, you accused me of not giving her enough attention. Now you tell me I shouldn't have brought her to the news conference. Make up your mind, Harriet. Which is it? My job is important, time-consuming. I can't run off and play with my children whenever the mood strikes me. They have to accommodate to my schedule as well."

"Damn you, Winston."

"Well, now there's a mature response. May I suggest we try to be civilized around each other?"

"You're not fit to be their father. I'm going to call my lawyer about the visitations."

Winston tented his fingers together, almost as if in prayer. "That wouldn't be a smart move, my dear. If you do that, I'll simply have to counter-sue and assume their physical custody."

"On what possible grounds?"

Winston leaned forward. "That you have placed them within the supervision of a highly suspect individual."

"What do you mean?"

"Agatha Stands, or whatever she calls herself, is not whom she says she is. It's an alias. You don't know anything about this woman. She could be a serial killer, a pedophile, an undocumented alien. Yet every day you leave that woman in charge of my children."

"Our children," Harriet corrected him.

"Precisely," he said. "Now, unless you have something else to say, I have matters of state to attend to." He began to shuffle the papers before him and resume reading.

Harriet stared at the ornate, metal letter opener on his desk. *It would be so easy to pick it up and ram it through his jugular.*

"No," said Opal inside of her.

"No, Mommy," said Justin even deeper down.

She got up.

"Please close the door on your way out," he said, not looking up from his papers.

During the drive home to Duxbury, Harriet's fingers kept opening and closing, strangling the car's steering wheel.

"Something's wrong," announced Opal upon seeing Harriet's face when she arrived home.

Harriet spoke sternly to Agatha. "I need to talk to you. Alone."

The two of them entered the small computer room and closed the door.

"And how was Mr. WcWhinnie?"

"I told you, he's not one to make idle threats. He says your name isn't really Agatha Stands."

"But it is my name, my true name, given to me by the Spirits when I did a hanbleciya, a vision quest. I only use the full version in ceremony."

"But Agatha Stands is not your legal name," Harriet pressed.

"No, it's not. My legal name is Agatha Rockefeller."

"From THE Rockefeller family?"

"In a manner of speaking, yes. Long time ago, the Indian agent had to account for families on the reservation, so he thought it amusing to assign names of famous people to our great-great-grandparents. That's why we go by our real names, the ones that the Spirits give us."

"Winston suggested that you were an illegal alien."

"He's the alien. My people were here on this continent long before his people, long before Columbus."

"But why do you want me only to pay you in cash?" Harriet continued. "Are you're running from the law?"

"All these questions. If you don't trust me, I'll leave." Agatha headed for the door.

"No, wait. He does that to people."

"He makes you doubt yourself, Harriet."

"He's good at that. He suggested that you might be a serial killer or a pedophile."

Agatha put her hands on her hips. "What do you think, Harriet? What did you say to him about that?"

"He threatened to take the children away from me." Harriet knew she sounded defensive.

"So you let him walk all over you?" In disgust, Agatha turned her back to Harriet, placing her hand on the door knob.

"Agatha, you're the best thing that has happened to this family in a long time. Stay. I need you to stay. Please."

Slowly, Agatha dropped her hand from the door knob. "No more questions. I'm a private person. Eventually, I'll tell you everything you need to know. I'd never hurt those kids. I love them. They're part of me now. They're my relations." She turned around and looked at Harriet.

Harriet was surprised to see tears brimming in Agatha's eyes. They had come to the brink of parting, and both of them were backing down. "I don't want you to go," she whispered. "Besides, Mom would kill me if you left."

"I'll stay as long as I can," Agatha said.

At that moment, they both knew that their contract had just been renegotiated. *As long as I am needed* had been dropped from Agatha's promise.

It was the price Harriet had to pay for not standing up to Winston McWhinnie.

As the weather turned its hoary face toward Spring and the sun called out to the winter-worn inhabitants, Sola developed a new and disturbing behavior. After her school bus would deposit her at Two Cranberry Lane, she'd occasionally go back outside and wander. At first, Agatha thought the girl was simply trying to ground herself in the noisy silence of Nature, but that wasn't the case. Sola would don headphones and play her music as loud as possible to drown out the inner voices.

It was quite unlike the occasional roaming of Opal, always followed by the dog in search of treats. Agatha had solved the problem of Opal's meanderings by placing a lock high up on the front door. It didn't occur to the old woman to try other routes of escape.

Not so with Sola. If the front door was locked, she'd slip out the side patio door.

This time, Agatha decided to follow her.

Talking loudly to herself, Sola marched up Cranberry Lane, turning into a neighbor's walkway. Without any hesitation, she entered the neighbor's house through a back door. Agatha waited, wondering what to do. Did Sola know these people? *If I scramble in after her, sure as shootin', someone's gonna accuse me of being a thief.* She stood outside and loudly whispered, "Psst, Sola."

Agonizing minutes passed by. Sola finally emerged, clutching a framed photograph of the neighbor's family. Apparently, the homeowners were absent.

"That's not yours, Sola. What are you doing, going into somebody else's house without asking?"

Sola hugged the framed photograph to her chest. "It's mine," she said. "It's my family."

"Give it to me."

"No, I won't. It's my house. It's my family." Sola lashed out at Agatha with her free hand and lost her balance. She tumbled to the walkway, the photograph falling against the concrete, its glass smattering to pieces.

"Come, Sola, let's go home." Agatha helped her up.

Sola pushed her away and stumbled back toward Two Cranberry Lane. Upon entering the McWhinnie house, she ran around locking all the doors.

Agatha retrieved the house key from her pocket and opened the front door.

Sola ran upstairs, screaming, "You're trying to hurt me."

"Looney tunes," announced Luna, emerging from her own room.

"I'm not crazy," yelled Sola from her bedroom.

"Don't bother her, Luna. I have to go clean some broken glass. Keep an eye on your sister and little brother. I'll be right back."

Agatha retrieved a broom, a trash bag, a pen, a piece of paper, and exited the front door. She swept up the debris on the neighbor's walkway and left a note, stating that Harriet McWhinnie would explain why the family photograph was missing and in need of repair.

As she neared the McWhinnie house, she could see the front door standing wide open. Digger was sitting alongside the driveway embankment.

"Digger, what are you doing?"

The dog slapped his tail on the gravel. A voice rose up from the embankment. "Oh, I'm so glad you're here."

Agatha peered down the embankment.

Opal was sprawled across the licorice mint. "I fell and couldn't get up."

Agatha dropped the broom, angled down the slope, and raised Opal to her feet, brushing wet leaves off her back.

"Where were you going, Grandmother?" Agatha asked.

"I wanted to see if the daffodils were up yet."

"Wrong patch. You found the mints instead. The daffodils know that winter isn't through with us yet." She helped the old woman back into the house, stopping at the kitchen refrigerator to retrieve a piece of chicken.

It was the least she could do for Digger.

His arms full of a dozen roses, Tom Breslin arrived that night to collect Harriet for dinner. Digger launched himself upon the burly man before he had even managed to place two feet within the foyer.

"Digger, down!" yelled Harriet from the kitchen. She emerged into the foyer, straightening her hair and wearing a red dress that complimented her figure. "Excuse my dog's rudeness." She pulled Digger off him.

Tom handed her the roses, then reached down and ruffled the Sheltie's hair. Digger was beside himself, moaning in pleasure. He turned his rump toward Tom as if to say, *Scratch here, please, please oh pretty please.* From an upstairs room came the sound of muffled voices and giggling.

Harriet retrieved a vase and water for the roses. "I'm sorry that I wasn't quite ready for your arrival. The hospital called to cancel Sola's appointment with the pediatric neurologist, second time in a row. We're getting kind of desperate here."

He followed her into the kitchen. "Where are the kids?"

Harriet looked away. "I banished them to an upstairs bedroom until after we left. I didn't want to scare you on our first real date."

After helping Harriet put on her coat, Tom ambled over to the staircase and announced in a loud voice. "Anybody up there? My name is Tom Breslin, and I sure would like to meet Harriet's family."

A door flew open. The first to emerge was Opal in day clothes and bare feet. She leaned over the bannister on the second floor landing. "Glad to meet you Mr. Breslin."

Oh Mother, thank heavens you aren't naked. Harriet smiled.

Justin peered through the white bannister posts. He waved down at Tom.

"Why, you must be little Justin," said Tom.

"I'm going to be six soon."

"Isn't it interesting how youth is always looking forward, while we're always trying to—"

"Tread water," suggested Harriet, buttoning her coat.

"At my age," Opal offered, "people are always saying 'My, don't you look good,' but it's a damn lie."

Luna and Sola appeared at the edges of the upstairs gathering.

"The twins," announced Harriet.

"Different as . . ." Tom searched for the right phrase.

"Day and night," answered Luna. "It's an old story."

"And each one beautiful in her own way," he added.

"Hi," said Sola. "I think you're a kind man."

"She must be the one with special insight," he murmured to Harriet.

Luna disappeared for a second then returned, dragging Agatha out onto the second floor landing. "This is Agatha, although we have to call her Miz Stands."

Agatha raised a hand in salute to Tom.

Tom turned toward Harriet. "So this is the miracle worker, the one you've told me about on the telephone."

Harriet nodded.

Tom looked back up at the clan gathered on the landing. "I'm honored to have met you all. I look forward to getting to know you better."

He opened the front door for Harriet and let her pass, then turned and gave them each a wave before shutting the door.

"Nice man," said Opal.

"He's got stubby fingers and a big face. Makes you wonder if there are any brains behind it." Luna let go of Agatha's hand.

"A kind man," said Sola, retreating back to her bedroom sanctuary.

Agatha started down the stairs, dinner preparations on her mind. "Appearances don't matter that much, Luna, the older you get. Your mother deserves to find a man of good heart."

"But then Daddy can't come home." Justin's forehead wrinkled with worry.

Luna knelt down in front of him and wiped the bangs off his face. "Sweetie, Daddy's not coming home. Ever. The sooner you understand that, the better off you'll be."

"But . . ." he started to protest.

"But nothing," continued Luna. "Miz Stands is right. Mommy needs someone who can love her back."

"I love Mommy."

"Of course you do. I love her too, although she sometimes doesn't know it. She spends a lot of time taking care of us, Justin. We need to let someone take care of her, don't you think?"

Justin nodded, as if in agreement, but he didn't like the truth of it one single bit.

FOURTEEN

A huge Nor'easter swarmed up the coastline, blanketing the Boston area with eighteen inches of new snow. Everything outside hushed to the soundless swirl of wind-swept flakes. Everyone inside hovered by their cozy fireplaces. In the seaside town of Duxbury, it became difficult to distinguish between the icy firmness of land and the sluggish fluidity of the ocean. Time slowed to a crawl.

The kids were delighted by a day off from school. Even Harriet was told to stay home and not risk driving in to work. She cooked up a pot of chili and made grapenut pudding for dessert. Much to her delight, Tom Breslin showed up with his truck, his plow, and several snow shovels.

"C'mon Justin, here's a shovel," he said. "You too, Luna."

"I want to help," said Sola.

"Of course you do." Tom handed her a shovel. "Why don't you take the front walk?"

Sola didn't have the strength to do much but push around the snow before retreating indoors. Tom dug the path to the front door.

Luna was surprised at how easy it was to shovel snow after all her weight lifting. Justin spent most of the time jumping in and out of snow mounds.

"Do you know how to make a snow angel?" Tom asked.

Justin shook his head.

Tom let himself fall backwards onto the snow and waved his arms up and down to make the wings. "There, now you do it."

Parting the front window curtains, Opal watched them all frolicking. Agatha appeared with her winter jacket, mittens, knitted hat, and boots. "Grandmother, do you want to make snow angels too?"

"Absolutely."

Bundled up, Opal and Agatha joined them, letting themselves fall backwards onto the white powdery fluff as it swirled around them. Then Harriet gently pushed Sola outside again. Everybody was laughing, making angels, pitching snowballs, until their noses turned cherry red and their fingers grew numb with the cold. Barking, Digger danced around the fallen angels.

"I lost my mitten," complained Luna. "Anybody seen it?"

They peered round, but no one could find it.

"Hot cocoa," announced Harriet. They all trundled inside, slapping snow off their boots and jackets, rubbing their hands together for warmth.

"Snow's falling even harder," said Opal eyeing Tom. "You may have to spend the night."

"My truck can make it through any storm. Unfortunately." He winked at Harriet.

Luna took a quick sip of her cocoa and stomped back outside to find the lost mitten. Digger ran after her.

The gusts of sea-borne wind pitched the snowflakes into a frenzied dance so dense that no one in the house noticed a black car creeping up the street. A man slowly emerged from the idling car, his face covered by a ski mask. He trudged toward the McWhinnie mailbox.

Coming around the back of the house, Luna and Digger both spied the man checking out their mailbox. He was sifting through their mail, looking for something.

"Hey," yelled Luna.

Holding onto an envelope, the man dropped the rest of the mail and ran toward his car. Luna and Digger took off after him. Being more fleet of foot, the dog got there first and sank his teeth into the man's ankle.

"Ouch, get offa me," he screamed. He rammed his fist into the dog's side, releasing the bite.

"Don't you hurt my dog," shrieked Luna, launching herself in a fury at the man. He fell onto the snow, the girl on top of him. She landed several solid blows onto his face and neck.

Snarling, Digger rebounded and tore at the man's hand. He dropped the envelope and, with his one free hand, pushed Luna to the side and scrambled to his feet. After kicking Digger loose, the man jumped into his car and hit the accelerator. In the snow, the car skidded from side to side before finally catching purchase. Luna sighted, then recited, the license plate number.

She retrieved the envelope. It was addressed to Agatha. After collecting the rest of the mail scattered on the snowbank, she ran back to the house.

Due to the ferocious nature of the storm, it took some time for a patrol car to arrive at Two Cranberry Lane. The young deputy flipped open a pad of paper and sat Luna down to ask her questions:

"What did the man look like?"

"His face was covered up. He was medium size," Luna answered.

"He assaulted my daughter," added Harriet.

"Will he come back?" asked Justin.

"I doubt it," said the deputy.

"Here's the license plate number. Luna was able to get a good look at the car." Tom handed a slip of paper to the policeman.

"Are you all right? Did he hurt you?" The deputy couldn't see any evident damage.

"Interfering with the mail is a federal crime," offered Opal. "I think you should call in the FBI."

"I'm not guilty. I didn't do it," said Sola.

"So, he was trying to steal a letter, you say?" The deputy continued writing notes, having appeared at the McWhinnie house several times when Sola had made 911 calls.

Luna nodded.

"Did the letter have any money in it?"

"No, it was a personal letter. I gave it to Miz Stands."

"Our live-in help," explained Harriet. "Where has she gone?" Agatha had disappeared when the deputy had first arrived.

"Well, I'll find out who owns the car. Anything else that you could tell me?" the deputy asked.

"Yes," said Luna. "Digger bit his left ankle and right wrist. I think he may have a couple of bruises on his face." A certain amount of pride shimmered in her voice.

"He's my dog," she added, rubbing the Sheltie's head.

"Okay, then. Try not to go out driving in this storm," said the police officer. "It's not safe out there." Harriet showed him out, then returned to the family conference.

"Given what's happened, I think I better stay the night," said Tom.

"Good idea." Opal's eyebrows shot up. "And I know exactly where you can sleep."

"Mother," scolded Harriet, "that's enough."

"He's my hero," said Luna, bending down and wrapping her arms around Digger. "Tonight, Digger, you're going to sleep in my room."

"To each his own," added Opal.

Over dinner, there was great excitement in the retelling of the day's events. Everyone had their own ideas.

"He was a monster," said Justin, "with claws and big teeth."

"A vampire," added Sola.

"No. It was a man after our mail. Maybe he'd written Miz Stands a nasty letter, and he felt bad about it." Luna knew all about poison pen letters, having penned several herself in the recent past. Once sent, it's the devil to get them back.

"Agatha, have you been rejecting any suitors lately?" asked Harriet.

"Beats me," Agatha answered. "But I've seen that black car hanging around here before."

"Mommy," said Justin, anxiety curling through his voice.

"It's okay, honey. Remember, Digger will protect us," said Harriet, hoping to stifle further discussion. "Tom, why don't you tell the kids about yourself?"

"Have you ever met a vampire?" asked Sola.

Harriet rolled her eyes.

"Something much worse," Tom answered.

That got everybody's attention.

"The wonderful thing about monsters and vampires is that they live outside. They're not part of us. They're just scary things that go creep in the night across the dark fields of our imagination." He looked at Harriet, sitting next to him at the dinner table.

"What's far worse," he continued, "is when there's someone you know, someone you love who's done a terrible thing."

"Like what?" asked Luna.

Tom paused, not sure whether to proceed. He looked at Harriet who nodded in confirmation. "Do you remember that case in the newspaper about the man whose son turned him in for murder?"

"The snitch," said Luna.

Tom grimaced. "Well, you're looking at him."

Luna's mouth dropped open. "You?"

Tom nodded. "Yes. I'm that son who still loves my dad even though he did an unspeakable act. He took the life of another human being. For nothing. For money and money is nothing."

"You're the social worker?" asked Sola

"I thought you looked familiar," said Opal.

"You knew about this, Mom?" asked Luna.

Harriet nodded. "Agatha told me the first time she saw him. She recognized him from the trial."

"Otherwise, I probably wouldn't have brought it up so soon. But you're bound to know." Tom shot a glance at Harriet.

"Does your Daddy love you?" asked Justin.

Tom bit his lower lip. "Eventually, he will."

"What about your brother, the police officer?" asked Luna.

Tom's face fell into a place of pain. Under the table, Harriet picked up his hand and squeezed it.

"It must hurt a lot," said Sola.

"There's a lot of grief. I miss my brother. You do what you think is right, but that doesn't protect you from the hurt. Leon thinks I'm a traitor to the family, that I should have protected our father."

"What about your Mom?" asked Justin.

"She's no longer alive, thank heavens."

"That's enough questions, kids. It's hard for Tom to talk about it," said Harriet.

"But I have one more question to ask." Luna's face had been stricken with anxiety during this conversation

"Go ahead. Ask," he said.

Luna bent over the table. "Was it worth it? When you turned him in, it broke up the family. You lost your father. You lost your brother. Would you do it again?"

"I've lost a lot. You're right about that. But what kind of person would I be if I let another man's life go to waste because I couldn't deal with my own grief? Loss is part of life. We're all missing someone or something. We make choices. We either stand on what's really important or we seal ourselves away into little cocoons."

"Like the undeveloped butterfly," echoed Agatha.

"I love my father. I love my brother. It wasn't an easy decision."

Perhaps it was her maternal instinct. Or his compassion for her family, arriving in the middle of the snowstorm with a plow.

Perhaps it was simply respect for the man and his sense of justice. Or his simple honesty. Whatever it was, Harriet knew that soon she would take this man into her bed and hold his grief in her arms for as long as it took.

A knock upon the apartment door. Winston put down his drink, wondering if Caitlin had finally come to her senses and returned. Banging on the door, however, was the man whom he mentally referred to as Sam Spade. Winston quickly opened and shut the door behind them. As the fellow limped into the living room, ice particles shucked off his pant legs like bleached pieces of corn. Dirty footprints from his torn boots laid claim to the white carpet.

"Nice place."

"I thought I told you never to come here."

The man paid him no heed. "I'm thinking that you owe me a lot more money than was agreed upon."

"Look," said Winston. "I asked you to investigate the identity and history of a single woman. Now how difficult could that be?"

"I got these boots new. Look at them. Goddam dog chewed them up. Look here." He pointed to his cheekbone and eye socket, red and bruising. "I got messed up some."

"At my Duxbury house?"

"Yeah."

Winston chuckled. "Don't tell me that my ornery mother-in-law gave you that shiner, because I know it wasn't Harriet. She doesn't believe in violence."

"The dog. The girl. You said it'd be easy. Nothing easy 'bout it. I didn't bargain on getting hurt. I could have roughed her up some, would have done her some good."

Winston glared at the man. "If I hear another threatening word drop from your mouth, you'll be sorry. That's my daughter you're talking about."

"Best you pay me double then. I don't take kindly to being hit. Makes me want to take revenge, you understand?"

It was blackmail, pure and simple. But Winston could tell from the brutish glimmer in the man's eye that he meant what he said. Better to pay the devil his due and get rid of him. He was sorry to have ever employed the thug.

"I've got a couple hundred in cash here," said Winston. "That'll have to do, because after tonight, I don't ever want to see your face again. Agreed?"

The man shook his head. "Your little Miss might have seen the license plate of my car. I've got to pull a disappearing act for awhile. Go up north along the coastline."

That's a relief, thought Winston.

"So, a couple of hundred ain't going to cut it. But I'll take that fancy gold watch you're wearing plus the cash. We'll call it quits then."

Winston whipped off the Rolodex watch and dug out the money from his wallet and handed them over to the man.

"You forget about my daughter," ordered Winston, "or else I'll come after you."

"I ain't gonna touch her," the man answered, limping out of the apartment. He was way too smart to physically retaliate against a minor child. Revenge can be sweet, but it has to be smart. It has to be done right.

FIFTEEN

The truth of a New England winter is that if the roads are impassible in the afternoon, by next morning they're usually clear. Tom slipped out of the house at dawn in order to maintain a discretionary silence about exactly where he had spent the night in the McWhinnie home.

Harriet awoke refreshed and relaxed. It would be a short workday for her, as she had previously arranged to collect Sola for a rescheduled doctor's appointment. She handed Agatha the Science Museum pass and whispered, "Take Mom to the interactive section. It'll stimulate her mind."

After Agatha, Opal, and the kids had all departed, the only one remaining at the McWhinnie house was Digger. As the day was chilly but not very cold, Harriet had attached him to the running line outside, leaving him a bowl of water and a dried pig's ear to chew on the porch.

When Agatha and Opal returned in the mid-afternoon, Digger was nowhere to be found. The running line dangled limp, no collar or dog attached. Round and round the neighborhood, Agatha and Opal drove, calling out, "Here Digger! Here boy!" Several times they stopped and asked pedestrians if they had spotted the dog.

No one had seen him.

Agatha called the pound.

He wasn't there.

"Where could he have gone?" she asked.

"Dogs wander," said Opal.

"Not Shelties," said Agatha. "Especially one with a collar still on him. It worries me."

She expected Justin or Sola to be the most affected by the news, but it was Luna who took it the hardest.

"He's my hero, my dog. I've got to find him." Luna took off on foot, searching the neighborhood.

"Will he come back?" asked Justin.

"If he can," answered Agatha.

Toward dusk, Harriet and Sola arrived.

"Digger's gone," announced Justin.

"The nurse took my blood," said Sola. "It hurt when she kept jabbing me."

"Honey, she didn't mean to hurt you. It's because you have such small veins." Preoccupied, Harriet muttered, "Where did he go?"

Just then, the front door flew open. Digger's collar jingled in Luna's hand.

"You found him?" shouted Justin.

"No. I stopped by our mailbox. This was stuffed in the back with his license and identification tags. Now, we'll never get him back," moaned Luna.

"Someone stole that dog," opined Opal.

"I'll call the police. We'll find him," said Harriet, her words sounding hollow even to herself.

"But why would anyone take Digger?" asked Luna.

"Daddy didn't even want him," added Sola.

"It was the monster. The monster got him," answered Justin.

The man drove north several hours, well into an area of the Maine highlands visited only by loggers and hunters. In the back of his car sat Digger, muzzled and looking out the window. The car bounced down a rutted, country road that led into deep woods. It was dark out, the only light being from the headlights.

"Yup, this'll do," he said, killing the engine. There was no one in hearing range.

Digger's tail thumped with excitement at the end of the journey, ready to escape the confinement of the back seat.

The man pulled out a pistol and checked to see if it was fully loaded. Then he opened the rear door. "C'mon, let's go," he said.

Out jumped the Sheltie, but instead of taking off, Digger stood there, looking at the man with his soft, almond eyes. He wagged his tail.

"I ain't gonna be friends with you, no way," said the man. "Remember you bit me, and my ankle still hurts." He raised his pant leg to show the dog. "So don't go begging for mercy from me, 'cuz you ain't gonna get any. Now git." He raised the pistol.

But "git" sounds like "sit," so Digger promptly sat down on the ground.

"Shoo." The man waved a hand at him.

Digger raised his paw for a "shake."

The man rubbed his head. "I can't shoot you if you keep acting that way."

Digger cocked his head, trying to understand what the man wanted.

"Hell, you're gonna die up here, anyways. If the coyotes don't get you first, then hunger and thirst will, 'caz you ain't getting anything with that muzzle on you. Why waste a good bullet?" He climbed back into the car and slammed the door shut. He backed the car around, then gunned the engine. One last look in his rear view mirror before turning a corner. That dumb dog was still sitting there, waiting for someone to tell him what to do.

Around the McWhinnie dinner table, they all sat in a glum silence, eating leftover chili. It just wasn't the same without Digger begging for food under the table.

"What did the doctor say?" asked Opal.

"The pediatric neurologist took a blood sample. He thinks that Sola may have a genetic disorder. Only blood tests will tell." Harriet picked at her food.

"What's a genetic disorder?" asked Sola. "Am I crazy?"

"Yes," said Luna. "Certifiable."

"Is it so difficult for you to be kind, Luna? If you had to live a day in Sola's shoes, you'd drive us all crazy." Harriet pushed her plate away, stood up, and left the table before she uttered words she might regret.

"Grandma, what's a genetic disorder?" asked Sola.

"When your father and mother made you, they each gave you a strand of their own DNA. The building blocks of all living tissue are the intertwining pairs of DNA strands. Sometimes, something crucial gets left out." Opal hoped that simple explanation would suffice.

"I don't understand," said Sola. "What got left out? Am I missing something?"

Digger expected the man to come driving back any minute, to remember what he had forgotten. But when the man did not return, Digger got up to explore a multitude of surrounding smells. The only one he recognized was that of Mouse. Nose to the ground, he discovered the recent scat of some large animal, one to avoid. The grumbling of his stomach told him it was past time for his supper. He trotted down the country road in the same direction of the car's departure. A slight wind shivered through the tall pines, rustling their needles as the darkness grew long shadows. Uneasy, Digger shifted into an easy trot to minimize the sounds of his traveling.

In the early evening, Agatha drove to the camp of Eagle Wing Woman and presented her with the gift of tobacco, wrapped in red cloth. "I need help to find someone who's missing," she said. "Here is his collar. It was taken off him when he was kidnaped. I want to know if he is alive or dead and how to find him."

The medicine woman ran her fingers up and down the collar. She then smudged the two of them with burning sage and placed a sprig of the Artemisia Silver Queen behind her left ear. Holding her rattle in one hand, the collar in another, she knelt down on a deerskin and began singing. She closed her eyes.

Underneath her closed lids, the eyes of Eagle Wing Woman searched the darkness. Finally she grew silent, except for an occasional grunt or nod of her head. Agatha held fast to the vision of Digger running free.

The medicine woman opened her eyes. "They say he isn't hurt, that he's trying to find his way home. He's far away and all alone. Like in another state. They showed me lots of woods, northern woods."

"Will he make it home?"

Eagle Wing Woman shrugged her shoulders. "I guess that's up to him, to you, to whomever else is searching for him. I asked your wolf medicine to protect him, to help you find him. This is the time for you to use what I've been teaching you. Pay attention to your medicine."

Agatha nodded. It would have to do. The image of northern woods suggested that Digger had been taken to Vermont, New Hampshire, or Maine. It was a large territory to cover. Digger didn't have much experience of being on his own. At least, he wasn't yet dead. She wanted to get to him before the prowling coyotes, hungry mountain cats, lumbering bears, and sub-zero cold.

But first, Agatha thought she should pay Winston McWhinnie a visit.

"Are you sure you want to do this?" asked Travis. "He's a powerful man and could make your life miserable."

"He already has. Did you see Luna's face after she had called the animal shelters? No trace of that dog anywhere. Her heart is breaking. Digger's become her dog. That man left the collar in the mailbox to send us a message."

"Revenge is one of the oldest human motivations."

"The guy was snooping around my mail. Same black car that had been parked before across the street. The only one I know who's interested in personal information about me is Harriet's ex-husband and you."

Travis smiled. "Guilty as charged. But I figure if you and I drive around those northern woods looking for a lost dog, we're going to get to know each other a whole lot better."

"I've got my own truck. I don't need you to chauffeur me around."

"Agatha, sometimes you've got to let others help you. You're too independent for your own good. Now, I'm not going to ask for any favor in return from you, except that you be appreciative and adore me." Travis looked straight ahead, a glimmer of a smile cracking at the corner of his lips.

"I'm not used to depending on others," she said.

In an authoritative voice once reserved for the judicial bench, Travis said, "Sure as shooting, you're going to fall in love with me."

It was an assertion to which Agatha could find no immediate objection.

Following Luna's directions, Travis drove Agatha to Winston McWhinnie's apartment building. She pushed the buzzer long and hard, hoping it would grate on his ears.

"Yes," he answered through the intercom. "It's late and unless this is Caitlin, contact me in the morning." The voice was husky, tinged with whiskey.

"No, it's Miz Agatha Stands, and I need to talk to you about your children."

"Are they all right? Come on up." He buzzed her through the front door. She signaled Travis to wait for her in the car.

She rapped hard upon his apartment door. Hair mussed by sleep, Winston opened the door in a rumpled bathrobe. "C'mon in. Now tell me what's the matter with the children? Is it Sola?"

"You haven't heard then?"

"What?"

"Luna is devastated."

"Are you going to tell me what happened or do I have to play Twenty Questions with you?"

Agatha entered his living space, taking in the expensive elegance and organized emptiness of the place in contrast to the chaos and liveliness of Two Cranberry Lane. She wanted to catch him off-guard.

"That man you sent—"

"What man?"

"The investigator who was looking through my mail."

"I don't know what you're talking about," he answered, turning his back on her to get a glass. "Are we getting paranoid here?"

"The man whom your daughter tackled, whom your dog bit on the hand and ankle."

"My daughter hit someone?" His voice betrayed him, the lack of surprise erased by foreknowledge of the event. He knew it. She knew it.

"He's not my dog anymore."

"No," agreed Agatha. "He's Luna's dog but he's disappeared."

"Run away then?"

"The man, the one you say you don't know, took him. He left the collar in the mail box. It was a message to your daughter that he could come in the middle of the night and take her too."

"He better not. I'd go after him if he did." Winston's jaw muscles clenched in anger.

"But since you don't know this man, how could you find him?"

They looked at each other with hostile, honest looks.

Both understood he was lying.

Agatha broke the silence. "Luna's heart is broken. Perhaps you could tell me where I might look for Digger."

Winston looked away. He poured himself a small glass of whiskey. With his back turned to Agatha, he answered, "If it were me, I'd start looking in Maine first."

"Maine," repeated Agatha, wanting to make sure she heard it right.

"But then again, if it were me, I wouldn't look at all. I'd simply say 'good riddance' to that scatterbrained fur ball." He sipped at the whiskey.

"You already did," said Agatha, walking to the front door to let herself out. "But it isn't Digger that I'm going to retrieve."

"Oh?"

"It's your daughter's heart."

SIXTEEN

"Edgar, what do you think I should do? I can't stay here forever." Opal leaned against the upstairs bedroom window. Outside a fierce wind blew, bending the barely budding trees, their branches flapping like arms begging for help. She cocked her head, listening to the roaring gusts.

"Will there come a time when I can no longer make a choice? Oh, I miss you, Edgar. You were my sounding board, my confidante. You used to snuggle up behind me in bed with those knobby knees of yours. Your hand was like a steam shovel, sweeping under me and pulling me into you. How I miss those bony knees. I know you're hearing me, Edgar. I can feel you around me, so why don't you ever show yourself?"

Opal looked around her room, taking comfort in all the familiar objects from her life with Edgar: the red velvet couch, the oriental rug, the rocking chair, the book shelf, the photographs of her grandchildren. *A comfort and a prison*, she thought. "It seems the older we get, we're required to compress ourselves into smaller and smaller spaces. Remember the big house, my favorite one, with four bedrooms and that mahogany staircase? Then came the single level, conventional house. Finally when the yard became unmanageable, you insisted on that two bedroom box of a condominium. But then you left me, so here I am in this one bedroom. When I'm consigned to a nursing home, I'll possess only half a room. I know, I know. You'll say it's still better than the cramped confines of a coffin."

She ran her hand along the lace curtain. "Edgar, why did you leave me? I thought love meant we'd always be together." Her hand let the curtain drop back into place, partially obscuring the view. "I know you have to run along now. Go then, my dear friend."

Her fingers bent in a subtle wave, as her eyes turned away from the curtained veil to the solid remnants of an old life.

At the breakfast table, the family held a council meeting with regard to Digger.

"Mom, I can't go do my homework or go to classes for thinking about him. My stomach is killing me," said Luna. "I can't eat or sleep."

Agatha regarded Luna with concern. *Was the girl unraveling into old behaviors? Was she sticking fingers down her throat again?*

"I don't know what else we can do that we haven't already done, darling." Harriet shook her head. "You've called all the local pounds. The police traced the car license, but the driver is nowhere to be found. If Digger doesn't show up in the next week, I think—"

"No! I don't want to hear it!" shouted Luna. "You're going to tell me he's gone forever. I refuse to accept that." She pushed away from the table, threw down her napkin, and stood up. "He's my dog. I'll find him."

"Of course, you will," said Opal.

"Mother, don't encourage her. Luna, you're almost an adult now. Sometimes things don't turn out the way you want them to."

"Like you and Daddy?" interjected Justin.

Harriet ignored that comment. "You have to be realistic. It doesn't mean we'll stop looking, but it's very likely that Digger isn't going to return."

"No," said Sola, shaking her head. "Digger's going to come back."

Somehow, it was all a déjà vu, like the time when the children learned that Winston and Harriet were getting a divorce. Try as they might, they couldn't stop the inevitable break. Even then, they ganged up on her, telling her that Daddy was coming home, coming back to them, to have faith. Well, faith didn't work any wonders for the McWhinnie marriage. She had to confront them with the bruising truth. Only then could they move on with their lives.

"You have to eat, sleep, and go to school, Luna. When life gets hard, you can't stop living. Digger may very well be dead by now." There, she said it. She put that idea out for them to digest.

"No, no!" cried Justin.

Luna glared at her.

Sola started weeping.

Opal's forehead wrinkled in disapproval, but she knew better than to openly contradict her daughter in front of the children.

"He's alive," announced Agatha in a soft voice.

All the McWhinnie heads whipped around towards Agatha.

"I think he's in Maine," she continued. "I'm taking a few days off to find him."

Harriet's mouth dropped open. "How do you know? Has someone seen him?"

"In a manner of speaking, yes," Agatha answered.

"Really Agatha, it's simply not possible for you to suddenly leave. What am I to do with Mother?" Anger, contained, reddened Harriet's cheeks.

"Mom, she can go to the Senior Day Care Center, can't you, Grandma?" said Luna. "I can collect Justin at school and watch him until you get home from work."

"What about Sola?" Harriet's jaw set into a rigid line. "What if something happens?" *What if she goes wandering again into people's houses? What if she has a seizure? What if she calls the police and tells them that dead bodies are everywhere? Honestly, what could Agatha be thinking? No, it isn't possible to let her go off on some cockamamie mission to find Digger. Absolutely not.* All these thoughts assailed her, unspoken in front of dear, sweet Sola.

"Well, then ask Daddy if he can come here in the late afternoon. It's only going to be for a few days," said Luna.

"It'd be over your father's dead body, before he'd show up for a family crisis," answered Harriet.

Luna pushed away from the table, rummaged through the rolodex by the telephone, then dialed the phone.

A hush fell over the family as they listened to the one-sided conversation.

"Hi, this is Luna. Miz Stands needs to go to Maine for a couple of days to find Digger. Mom doesn't want us to be alone during the later afternoon. Do you think you can come over and stay with us?"

A pregnant pause.

"Thank you." Luna hung up the phone. She returned to the table, sat down, and picked up her fork. "He'll start tomorrow afternoon. Said for Miz Stands to take all the time she needs to get Digger."

Once again, Harriet's mouth fell open. "Your father said that?"

Luna popped a piece of meat into her mouth and shook her head.

"Well, then I don't understand," said Harriet.

Luna glanced at Agatha and grinned. "You told me that Daddy wouldn't do it, so I phoned Mr. Breslin instead."

"You called Tom?" asked Harriet.

Luna nodded and kept on eating.

"But—," Harriet started to object.

"That's what I call initiative," interjected Agatha.

"Or intrigue," added Opal. As her eyes locked onto those of her daughter, Opal's finger brushed past her lips, a subtle gesture telling her adult daughter in no uncertain terms that it was a good time to hush.

Despite a double coat, Digger had to keep moving in order to keep warm. While the cold wind blew damp and gusty in Duxbury, it chilled to the bone in Maine. Digger ran out of road while following his nose deeper into the woods. Even though he was hungry, it was mainly thirst that drove him on. He forded several ice-covered streams until he discovered a pond with some open water. Treading cautiously out onto the ice sheet, he dunked his muzzled mouth into the water, sucking up only a tease of water. He pawed at the leather guard, backed off the ice, and shook his head. Thirst was about to drive him crazy; it was making him weak.

But when his ears picked up a singular high yipping answered by an excited chorus of coyote song, his irritation faded. The howls worked themselves into a frenzy. They were nearby. Digger backed into a hollow tree stump, laying his head down on his paws. It was time to hide, to be quiet: his aggressive bravado and door attacks in Duxbury were nigh forgotten. The only portal in this wilderness was that which stood between life and death.

Agatha packed her knapsack: warm outdoor clothes, several flashlights, a sealed bag of venison sticks, a pouch of tobacco, her Native American pipe, and a knife. She emptied a coffee can of stray bills and tucked them in her wallet.

As she headed down to the second floor, Luna greeted her with Digger's collar and leash. "You're going to need these." She reached into her back pocket and pulled out her cell phone. "Take this too. Call me immediately when you find him. Promise?"

"I promise."

Before Agatha could descend the stairs to the first floor, Sola and Justin approached.

The boy thrust his teddy bear into her hands. "He'll give you big hugs."

"Okay, but I can't keep him forever. He'll need to come back to you when I return."

Sola took her hand. "Will you come back too?"

"What goes north must come south," Agatha answered.

At the bottom of the stairs stood Harriet and Opal. Handing her a wad of money, Harriet tried to apologize. "Here, you're going to need some money. I'm sorry to have doubted you. You'll call us when you find out about Digger?"

Agatha pulled out Luna's cell phone and nodded.

"I asked Edgar to go with you. He's got a good sense of direction," announced Opal.

"Mom," started Harriet, but Agatha interrupted before anything more could be said.

"If I get lost, Grandmother, I will certainly ask for Edgar's help." Agatha hoisted her knapsack, picked up her duffel bag, and left the house. Out in the driveway sat Travis, patiently waiting in his idling car.

As Agatha slid into the front passenger seat, he said, "Well, we're off on an adventure, Miz Stands. To Maine then?"

"To Maine," she answered.

"What part of Maine do we head to first?" *Maine is a really big state*, he thought.

Agatha studied the map, her finger tracing various routes. "Head north. The wolf will then tell us where to go."

"The wolf," he said, looking quizzically at her.

Toward downtown Boston, they drove northward in silence. Travis wondered about Agatha's sixth sense. *Was this going to be a wild goose chase? What did she mean by a wolf giving them directions?*

The only wolf he noticed on the trip was himself. *A wolf kept in check,* he laughed to himself. *Agatha was the kind of woman you had to approach slowly and with careful deliberation, else she might bite you.*

"What's so funny?" she asked.

"Do you know how crazy this trip is? Maine is a big place. The dog could be anywhere, in another state or another state of being. Yet here am I, the retired judge, happily chauffeuring you whither you want to go."

"You didn't have to come, Travis."

"Now don't be getting defensive with me, Agatha. I'm here because I enjoy your company. At seventy-one, I know the kind of woman I like. I'm plotting to get you alone in my arms at some forsaken Maine motel."

"Is that so?" She raised her eyebrows.

"Way I figure it, Maine is just too darn cold to sleep in a single bed."

"That's why I thought Digger could sleep with you when we find him." She kept looking straight ahead.

"You're a hard woman, Agatha Stands. A hard woman." His right hand inched over and grasped her left one. He pulled the back of her hand toward his lips and kissed it.

There was absolutely no resistance on her part.

SEVENTEEN

"Don't you like me just a little bit?" Jeffrey Porter touched Luna's hand.

It was like a snake had just bit her, so fast did she whip her hand back into her pocket. "Of course, I like you, but I don't love you. I don't want to make out with you. Why can't we just be friends?"

"You're afraid you'll get a reputation at school?" he asked. "C'mon. Just one little kiss." He wrapped his arm around her.

"No." She pushed him back. The pimples on his face disgusted her. She peeked around the woodshed at the McWhinnie back door.

"I'll drive you anywhere you want to go. C'mon, one kiss. I won't ask for anything more."

"Anywhere I want to go?" Luna got to thinking.

"I'll take you to your Dad's place."

"For a kiss, right*?*" *I can do it if I keep my eyes closed and my lips shut*, she thought.

"Yes. Anywhere," he answered.

"Okay." She grabbed his hands. *All the better to keep them from roaming.* Luna inhaled deeply, closed her eyes, and tilted her face toward him.

He wrapped their hands behind her back and pulled her close, grinding his lips down upon her mouth.

It hurt, and she needed to come up for air. As she started to pull away, he stuck his tongue into her mouth, breeching the barrier of her previously clenched teeth. One hand, now freed, grazed past her left breast. But it was the hip against hip movement that caught her off-guard, as they leaned against an outside wall of the McWhinnie shed.

The feelings of *shouldn't, don't want to, what is happening?* ran contrary to a liquid fire stirring inside her. It was as if the upper half of her wanted to extricate herself, whereas the lower half kept moving inextricably forward. Fire and ice, fire and ice, and she was melting fast.

Jeffrey had bargained for a kiss, unprepared for the global warming that followed. He couldn't resist running his hands, inside her jacket, up and down the lovely curves of the female body. His penis flagged at full staff but, luckily, was covered by his own long jacket.

What to do now? He kissed her again and thumped his body against hers, her legs slightly opened. He wanted to lay her down on the frost-hard ground and probe the mysteries of her body, but caution, age, and inexperience kept them both standing, swaying until release and relief let him step back from the precipice.

That momentary space jarred them back from the metamorphosis into mindless creatures of passion, their hard breaths intertwining in the cold air, followed by the sound of the back door banging against the house. Tom Breslin called, "Luna, Luna are you out there?"

He couldn't see her, thank God. She zipped up her jacket, straightened her blouse. "Remember," she said, before running back to the house, "You promised. Tomorrow afternoon, after school. I'll make an excuse. Take me to Boston."

Breathless, he nodded. It was the least he could do.

Opal didn't know what to make of Tom Breslin, who was sitting beside Sola, helping her with her homework while Justin assembled a puzzle on the floor. *Who was this man, anyway? Had she met him before? He seemed vaguely familiar. Such a large chest, a big open face.*

"Are you a friend of Edgar?" she asked.

"Who is Edgar?" He didn't remember Harriet having mentioned anyone by that name.

Opal didn't bother to answer but shuffled off and brought back some papers to him. "Are you a lawyer? I need to see someone about my will." The paper stack she handed him held hospital instructions for a home enema.

"No, I'm no attorney. Don't have much truck with them. I'm a social worker, a friend of Harriet's. In the summer, I take people on fishing trips in my boat."

"A sea captain?"

"Yes, that's right."

"On a ferry boat?"

"No," he answered. "Not a ferry boat."

"Across the river Styx," she added, "with the three-headed dog."

"That I'd like to see." He chuckled.

"A fairy boat," chimed in Sola. "With pink wings to fly into the mist."

"Charon. You're Charon," announced Opal. "Glad to meet you." She reached out to shake his hand.

"I'm Tom. Tom Breslin. My boat's a plain thing, not fancy. Sort of like me," he said, hoping to clear up the confusion. "Come Spring, I'll take the two of you out on it."

Opal shook her head. "Nope. I'm not ready yet."

"And everybody on that fairy boat would be perfect," said Sola. "They'd have no problems, no hurts, no pain. Everybody would be okay."

At that instant, Tom understood Harriet's sorrow. For if you can't heal a child, it's as if you've broken the compact between parents and children: that for a space of time, you will keep them safe, protect them, soothe their wounds, and then set them free. And if you can't heal a parent, what's left but to prepare him or her for the final passage?

Such a sad business, he thought. *But at least she's got Justin and Luna. Where is that girl, anyway? She went outside to talk to that boy some time ago. Best bring her in before she gets into trouble.*

He'd opened the back door and called out.

Digger heard an animal cry, not a threatening territorial sound, but a lonely tri-tone call, one canine to another. Thinking it might be another dog, the Sheltie headed in the southeastern direction. Another dog might bring the two-leggeds. They'd remove this contraption from his nose and feed him. His paws were growing rough with the constant traveling, sharp, frozen sticks jabbing into the pads from time to time. Unlike at home, where his tail rode high around any other dog, Digger kept his tail tucked low. He wanted to fade into the landscape, not provoke it to attack him.

Occasionally a mole or a chipmunk scurried across his path, but he couldn't kill them for the muzzle. Best to keep on moving. Squirrels chattered at him, tossing insults, but he paid them no mind. He was heading home, although he hadn't the slightest idea where home lay. Somehow, Digger had faith that home would eventually come to him.

That is, if the coyotes didn't find him first.

Mid-day, up the Maine coastline, Travis and Agatha stopped for a cup of lobster bisque and hot coffee. Agatha warmed her hands in the steam of the freshly brewed java.

"I've been thinking," she said.

"I'm all ears."

"Sometimes, you've got to believe in other human beings."

"I agree."

"Like you, for instance,"

"A most trustworthy fellow," he said.

"You once asked me if I was in trouble."

"I did."

"You see, I can't allow myself to love a man, unless I trust him, unless I know he loves me."

"Fair enough. I love you, Agatha. At my age, it doesn't take long to know if the magic is there or not."

"But I'm a private person with many secrets."

"Yes, you are."

"And you might not love me if you knew the worst of them."

Their relationship had come to a delicate crossroads. From his long judicial career, Travis knew the absolute power of secrets, often more damaging than the deed they were originally meant to conceal. Over time, secrets form scar tissue. Relationships tend to shred under the clutch and claw of what is not being said, the absence first of the particular, then of the whole person.

So Travis waited, knowing that Agatha had to make those choices for herself: to love fully or to keep her self apart.

"I came to the McWhinnie household on a whim, on a prayer. I was running away. I declared myself a person with no past and found myself in a house with no future."

"You've made a big difference to that family, Agatha."

Agatha waved away that remark. "Their problems allowed me to forget mine, at least until now." She lurched to her feet. "Shall we go look for Digger?"

Travis placed his hand upon hers. "Sit down, Agatha, I'm here to listen."

Agatha slumped back into her seat. "All right, but don't ever say I didn't warn you."

He encompassed her hand with both of his hands, not only to warm her, but to embrace her in the smallest gesture.

Agatha fortified herself with another sip of coffee. "I had to leave the reservation. It wasn't the police that frightened me. It was the way my relatives and my relations looked at me. Because of what I did," she stammered.

"Yes," said Travis, encouraging her to go on.

"I was married to a man who loved me. And then I wasn't anymore."

"You got divorced?"

"No," answered Agatha.

"Widowed then?"

"On the reservation," she answered, "I was known as the woman who poisoned her husband."

Digger had no reason to distrust human beings, although at times they were a strange lot. They couldn't speak his language much. Rather, he had had to adapt to their stunted forms of communication. He could sense what they could not, smell their fears, hear their whispers. Sometimes, he was reduced to beggar status around them, cold outside, while they warmed themselves by the fire on the inside. Other times, they walked blindly into his world, unaware of all the life scrabbling, sniffing, snorting, scrambling to get out of their way. As if they had forgotten that they, too, were part of the animal kingdom.

He heard the excited chatter of young voices before he sighted them. Out of the dark woods into the tawny field of wild grass, he turned in the direction of the human beings, sure they'd lead him home.

"Arsenic and Old Lace. It's a minor role for me, but fun," said the sandy-haired boy, traipsing through the field, his twenty-gauge shotgun gun slung over his right shoulder.

"You'll become a famous dude and forget all about hunting," teased the darker-haired boy.

Their eyes kept scouting for any movement. It wasn't exactly hunting season, and they didn't expect to find much. Maybe a squirrel, a hare, or a raccoon.

"I wish my Dad would let me have a twenty-two. He promised to take me deer hunting next winter."

"Look," whispered the second boy. "Did you see that?"

Into the blinding sun, they both squinted toward the far edge of the field.

"It's a fox," murmured the first boy, getting excited. He crouched low and crept forward.

The fox must have heard him for it stopped in mid-trot and glanced over in their direction.

The two boys shielded their eyes from the sun as they squatted lower. They brought their shotguns to their shoulders, sighting the prey.

The fox's ears shifted back and forth. His nose went up in the air, testing the scent. He turned as if to come in their direction, his color and shape shifting in the bright sunlight.

"Maybe he's rabid," whispered the sandy-haired boy. "'caz he seen us, and he's not running away."

"Don't let him get too close. Shoot!"

Their shotguns let forth a volley of bird shot at the fox trotting in their direction. Although their aim was skewed by the solar glare, they hit him in the right hind leg. The animal screamed in pain and pivoted in the air, sprinting away from the noise, the guns, and the boys.

"Did you get him?" the dark-haired boy asked.

"Yoweee! Didn't you see him jump?"

Untrained in the tracking of a blood trail, the boys didn't try to follow the wounded fox. It was time to go home, get fed, tell big tales of the one they almost killed.

On three legs, Digger stumbled and ran, blood seeping from his face to his haunch.

"Oh, I don't feel at all well," moaned Luna the next day. "My intestines."

"Oh my," said the principal. "Do you need to see a doctor?"

Luna shook her head. "It's an attack of borborygmus."

"That sounds serious."

"It won't last, but I need to go home and lie down."

"Of course, you do. I'll tell the teachers of your absence."

Luna left the school, smiling. Down a couple of blocks, she had arranged to meet Jeffrey at his car. She told him about her medical excuse.

"You lied to the principal?"

"No," she said, sliding into the passenger side of the car and slamming the door. "Borborygmus is a medical term for the growling sounds in the lower intestine, especially when you've eaten beans."

"Don't you dare fart in my car." He started up the engine. "Are we off to your Dad's place again?"

"Nope," said Luna. "We're going somewhere else."

Maybe, I'm going to get lucky. A terrifying but thrilling thought. He kept his eyes on the road and his ruminations to himself.

EIGHTEEN

Having cautioned Agatha not to say anymore in a public place, Travis paid the bill and hustled her outside to his car. "Now we have some privacy in which to talk. First, were you ever charged with the crime of murder?" He knew that his voice carried a lawyer's tone, but he couldn't help it.

"When I heard that the FBI were looking to question me—"

"The FBI?" *Why were the Feds after her?*

"It happened on the reservation. When it's something major, beyond the tribal courts, the FBI steps in. We're a sovereign nation within the United States."

"Right. I forgot. Stupid of me." *Listen you old fool. Slow down. She needs to take her time in the telling of it.* "Why don't I drive and you tell me all about it?"

Agatha shifted in her car seat, looked out the window, breathing in and out, very quiet. The air was pregnant, taut and tense, with an advancing front of snow.

Travis eased the car out into the line of traffic. Minutes rolled by. He regretted cutting off her confession, fearful that others might overhear her.

Agatha closed her eyes and tilted her head, as if listening. Finally, she said, "The wolf seems to be pointing west. We're not too far away."

"Right," he said. "I'll turn left at the next road." He looked at her, then outside, but couldn't discern any wolf.

Slowly, Agatha resumed the story. "After I graduated from high school, I left the reservation for Chicago. I was stupid then, forgetting everything my grandmother and my aunties had taught me. It was like I needed to understand my mother who had become a drug addict. I still went to pow-wows nearby, to get some of that fry bread and Indian tacos. Worked a mess of jobs, factory, small farm. Had a little house and a bunch of dogs and two broken-down cars in the rear."

He waited, knowing that background is context, a way of making meaning out of the extraordinary event.

"I was a loner, content to be by myself as long as I had a mess of library books. Nobody expected me to get married, but then I met Jesse. Or rather, we came back together at a big pow-wow. We knew each other from the time we were little kids. A tall big guy with hungry eyes and a wonderful mother. We'd lost track of each other after high school. He'd gone on to college, then business school on scholarship, while I was gathering all that life experience. He'd done really well, helping Anglos and reservation people understand each other. Made a lot of money too. We lived together 'bout eleven years. Then one night, he got a notion that we had to get married. Traditional wedding back on the reservation. It's what his Mom wanted."

At first, a singular flake spat on the windshield, then a multitude. The snow began to fall in earnest, straight dotted lines to the earth. Travis slowed at an intersection and turned westward. So quickly and quietly was the snow falling that his tires laid down new tracks in the lesser road.

"Were you happy?" he asked.

"Yes," she finally answered. "I loved Jesse. He loved me. But he got to a time in his life when he wanted to move back home to the reservation to be near his Mom. I didn't. I knew what was waiting there, being married to a handsome and successful guy. The people would take him away from me, first with their nibbling little demands, then with bigger and bigger projects. 'Jesse, only you can do this,' they'd say, gobbling up all his time and energy. As for me, it was the gossip about my dark skin. 'What does he see in her? She's no full-blood. She's no Indian.' I knew what was coming, and I was right. Reservations are big families that you love but don't really like. You know what I mean?"

He simply nodded.

"Jesse was the big man on the reservation, while I was the little fish in a pond of piranhas. My grandma was dead, my aunties had long left, and I was being chewed good. Jesse told me to pay them women no mind. I loved him. He was happy. But then the big, strong man got sick. He didn't want anyone to know. In the middle of the night, we drove to Chicago where the docs told him he had stomach cancer. That chemo business about killed him. Lost a lot of weight until I started giving him marijuana. He still didn't let anyone know what was happening. So the reservation women began whispering that I must be a bad cook or something."

The wind picked up, slamming the snowflakes onto the windshield. Travis slowed down. It was getting harder to see the middle line.

Agatha didn't seem to notice, so caught up in another time and place. "Then the pain began, mostly in the night. I knew he was dying. It got so bad one time, he said he was going to take his pistol and blow out the back of his brains. I hid his guns. I begged him to let me take him back to the hospital, but he didn't want to die in those sterile four walls, away from his people, his feet not being able to touch the Grandmother."

Agatha paused. "If I tell you the rest, can they use that against me?"

Travis smiled. "Not if you marry me."

"Are you proposing to me? Hell, we haven't even slept together."

"A situation I hope to remedy on this trip," he answered, pulling into a motel parking lot. The snow was falling fast, making driving nigh impossible.

The storm had come up suddenly. On the trail of the blood spoor, the coyote pack fanned out, noses to the ground. There was a wounded animal nearby. If they didn't catch their prey soon, they'd go hungry during the storm. The falling snow muffled their advance, while the blustery wind ruffled the fur on their necks. Normally, they wouldn't have been interested in another canine but the alpha female was pregnant. The den was nearby. The canine was an intruder. As soon as they could spot him, they'd rush in for the kill.

The hair on the back of Digger's neck rose. He couldn't see or hear the danger sneaking up behind him, but he could sense it. On three legs, exhausted and terrified, he lurched over the frozen terrain, heading he knew not where.

Downwind, the smell of Digger's panic mobilized the pack to come together in a full run. They burst out of a stand of pine trees. Through the wavy lace curtain of falling snow, they spied the canine.

He had stopped running and was standing there, facing them, black in outline against the drifting white of the storm. Bigger than they had anticipated. The coyotes spread out and moved ahead with deliberate speed.

The canine raised his head in a mournful, tri-tone howl, freezing the pack's forward momentum.

It was one thing to kill a wounded, domestic dog, but another to attack a large, healthy wolf.

Hearing the wolf howl, Digger kept moving, until he could run no more. He lay down in the snowed-over ruts of a logging road, panting, bleeding, and in pain. He knew that death would soon arrive. If the coyotes didn't disembowel him, surely the wolf would tear him into pieces. He closed his eyes to sleep, neither seeing nor hearing the pick-up truck slithering and sliding up the unplowed road.

If only I could have slept a full eight hours, thought Harriet. She rubbed her eyes, yawned, and walked to the hospital window. It was snowing heavily outside, but nothing would have kept her from the delayed appointment with the pediatric neurologist.

The receptionist showed her into the office of Dr. Thibeault. He arrived, breathless, his arms laden with files and reports which he dropped upon his desk. "Mrs. McWhinnie?"

Over the desk, they shook hands, then both sat down. Harriet kept kneading her hands together, a way of binding her anxiety.

"Did you find out what is the matter with my daughter?" She braced herself to hear the recitation of all the old, tentative diagnoses.

"Yes. The blood tests, especially the FISH test, show that she has VCFS."

"VCFS?" It was not one of the many psychiatric terms with which she was familiar. "Are you sure?"

"It's a definitive diagnosis."

A rush of relief surged through her. *After all these years, all these doctors, finally someone knows what is wrong with Sola. With knowledge comes the possibility of treatment.* "Is it a curable condition?" Harriet asked, crossing her fingers.

Compassion softened the doctor's academic facade. He shook his head. "VCFS is a genetic disorder. It stands for Velo-Cardio-Facial Syndrome. Also sometimes known as Shprintzen Syndrome, DiGeorge Sequence, Conotruncal Anomaly Face Syndrome, and the one I most prefer, Deletion 22q11.2 Syndrome. It is the most common micro-deletion syndrome, occurring in about one out of every two to four thousand births."

"Please, Dr. Thibeault, I don't understand," Harriet said. "I'm a financial advisor, not a biologist. Can you tell me what this means in lay terms?"

"I apologize. Let me explain. As you probably know, every child inherits two sets of genes, one from the mother and one from the father. These genes are bundled, compacted, and carried on the chromosomes. In the human body, there are twenty-two pairs of chromosomes, excluding the sex chromosomes. They interact with each other, sending messages back and forth. Do you follow me so far?"

"Yes, but is it something I did wrong when Sola was a little girl?"

"No, it happened much earlier than that. If you remember, from your biology class in high school, the chromosomes look like Xs, with the upper arms shorter than the lower arms. At the time of conception, when the sperm cell and the egg come together, they each contain a single copy of the twenty-three chromosomes. Together, they create a zygote, a single cell with twenty-three chromosomal pairs. At the moment of the combination of the sperm cell and the egg, sometimes there can occur a problem."

"Like what?" asked Harriet, listening very carefully.

"There can be a deletion in a particular chromosome, a missing part. In the case of your daughter, there is a deletion in the 22q11.2. What that means is that there is a small segment in the long arm of one copy of the twenty-second chromosome that is missing."

"Missing? But can't the other one, the complete chromosome, compensate for the incomplete one? We're all missing something or another in our lives, yet we can learn to offset our weaknesses with our strengths." It seemed like a good analogy.

Deep in thought, struggling to find the right words, Dr. Thibeault laced his fingers together, those of the left hand notched besides its corresponding twin on the right hand. "It all depends on the particular gene. Some singular genes can function properly; sometimes both genes are necessary. Let me explain further. Within each chromosome are these bundled genes. The genes are like textbooks, blueprints for the production of particular proteins that are necessary for cellular functions. When a part of that genetic code goes missing, then the human body, on a cellular level, lacks the information to develop a normal body. The deletion in the 22q11.2 produces, at last count, over one hundred and eighty-five abnormalities in the human body, some of which you have already seen in your daughter."

"The cerebral palsy."

"Yes. Also the cleft palate, the learning difficulties, the single kidney, speech difficulties, immune deficiencies, tapered fingers, the grand mal seizure, to mention a few."

"She's psychotic," added Harriet. "Some say she is schizophrenic." Suddenly the psychiatric diagnoses appeared friendlier, at least potentially curable.

"We know that schizophrenia has a strong genetic component, but your daughter's mental illness is caused by the deletion of a very particular segment on one copy of the twenty-second chromosome. It's complex. Some of the genes in the deleted area code for either high or low activity of a particular protein. If the functional gene of the normal copy of that chromosome codes for the low-activity protein, then these particular Deletion 22 children are more likely to develop hallucinations, phobias, psychoses, and a host of other symptoms of mental illness."

"But if the gene on the complete chromosome codes for a high activity protein, then what happens?" Harriet struggled to understand.

"Then the children have a lot of physical problems and learning disabilities but will probably not develop mental illness. Unfortunately, your daughter is one of those with the gene on the normal chromosomal copy that produces the low activity protein. Somewhere between twenty-five to thirty percent of these VCFS kids develop mental illness."

"Twice cursed then," groaned Harriet. It was beginning to dawn on her that if Sola's problems were at a cellular level, there wasn't any way to "cure" her.

"Knowing what we do now about the Deletion 22 Syndrome, there will be other tests we'll need to run on your daughter. Many of these Deletion 22 kids have congenital heart disease, due to malformations in the heart tissue. We'll also need to do an electrocardiogram, a renal ultrasound, ophthalmic exam, visual-spatial tests, a hearing evaluation due to her history of upper respiratory infections, and a brain MRI for our own research."

She heard the trail of his words, but her thoughts were elsewhere, skewed by an aching heart.

Oh, Sola, my baby. They'll want to prod and poke you, all in the name of science. A little patch here, a little patch there. But deep down, in the very foundation stones of your body, there is something missing. Something that threatens to tear down the whole house of who you are and who you have been.

Giving the missing link a name answered Harriet's need to know. She was relieved that, somehow, it wasn't something she did or didn't do that had brought all this suffering onto her daughter. On the other hand, the starkness of the diagnosis offered no hope that Sola's future would be anything but the present torment.

Harriet returned home to find Tom and Justin hard at work on a marble runway. Determined to let Sola know the diagnosis, Harriet wanted to reassure her that it wasn't a matter of her being a good or bad person. That plan, like so many others, backfired.

"If I can't be normal, I don't want to live," sobbed Sola, "You can't know, Mommy, how horrible it is to have all these voices inside, screaming at me. Why can't I be like Luna? I'll never fall in love, get married, have children, will I?"

The tears cascaded down her cheeks. She stood up, ran into her bedroom, slamming the door behind her.

If only Sola were retarded, it would be so much easier, thought Harriet.

Opal overheard the hushed conversation between her beleaguered daughter and tearful granddaughter. *My poor baby,* she thought. *I really should leave. Harriet has much too much to handle. Perhaps it's getting time for me to leave. Where has Agatha gone? She'd tell me if it was time.*

Opal looked around her comforting bedroom. *It'll be so hard to go away. Truth is, I'd rather stay here.*

The truck pulled up short. A heavy, jowly man in a red, wood cap slid out of the vehicle and ambled over to the inanimate Digger. "What do we have here? A dead animal?"

He looked closer, his breath spiraling in the air. At that moment, a snowflake fell on the dog's nose. It wrinkled in response.

"Nope, by God, you're still alive. What's that thing on your face?" He reached into his denim overalls and pulled out a Swiss army knife. Grabbing hold of the muzzle, he sawed the leather in half, then proceeded to a closer examination of the dog. "Man, somebody shot you up good. Bad aim, that's for sure. C'mon, I guess I'll take you home, clean you up some, see if we can bring you back to life."

With massive arms, he leaned down and scooped up the skinny dog who lay limp in his arms. "Better put you up front with me, before you freeze to death." He opened up the passenger side of the truck, gently nestling the dog on the bench seat.

Digger's eye flickered open, as the man started driving down the bumpy, snow-clogged road.

The man patted his head. "You've decided you're going to live after all, huh? The Missus gonna curse me for bringing you home. She calls me the Road Kill King. But you don't look dead to me. At least, not yet."

Digger fell back asleep. His paws twitched back and forth as he dreamt of snarling coyotes and howling wolves.

"I'm missing something here," said Jeffrey. "I thought you wanted to go to Boston to spend time with me."

"No," answered Luna. "I've arranged to meet someone. A friend."

She had directed him to an apartment building in Back Bay. He had fantasized, quite mistakenly, that she had a friend who was going to loan her the apartment for an afternoon. Instead, Luna was giving him instructions to return in an hour's time to pick her up.

"Is this friend a guy?" he growled.

"No. I won't take long." She leaned over and gave him a peck on his cheek, a mollifying gesture. "I really appreciate you helping me out on this."

Luna ascended the steps of the apartment building. She rang the buzzer for apartment 4B, then pushed the door open and walked up the four flights of stairs.

At the end of the hallway stood Caitlin by an open door. "How did you ever manage to get here without your family knowing?"

"It's always been easy for me to manipulate situations," answered Luna. "Only this time, I don't know what to do." She shrugged off her winter jacket in the living room.

Caitlin handed her a steaming cup of tea and sat down. "What makes you strong also makes you weak."

Luna shot her a puzzled look.

"Because when you always rely on your strengths," explained Caitlin, "you'll never pay attention to the less developed areas of yourself. You love him. So did I. It's easy for me to fall in love, but it's much harder to cut the cord and walk away."

"I can't. He's my Dad. He's family." *Without family, you're nowhere*, thought Luna.

NINETEEN

"One room or two?" asked the motel clerk, smiling at Travis and Agatha.

Travis deferred to Agatha.

"One," she answered.

Travis winked at her, a grin spreading over his face.

"A king or two doubles?" the clerk continued.

Once again, Travis nodded to Agatha to make the decision.

"Two doubles," she replied.

A little frown clouded his face.

The clerk took down his credit card information and then passed them only one key.

"We need two," said Agatha.

He produced another one.

En route to the motel room, she huffed, "Why do they always assume that the woman wouldn't want her own key?"

"He probably guessed that we wouldn't be going out in this snowstorm."

"We have to eat."

He opened the door and stepped aside to let her pass through. "There's a small family restaurant across the street."

She lay across both beds, testing their firmness, then chose the one farthest from the television set. "I'll take this one. Hasn't been fully broke."

"Nor have you," added Travis.

Agatha paid him no mind. "Let's get some dinner."

"Do I dare?" he asked, his eyes twinkling. Intuition told him that it was better to use humor with Agatha. Otherwise, he'd never hear the rest of the story.

Outside the motel room, the gusting wind yanked at their coats. By the time, they had crossed the street to the restaurant parking lot, the snow had frosted their hair.

"We look like two ghosts skulking in the dark," said Travis.

Agatha stood still, holding her hand up to Travis to be quiet. "He's moving farther away."

"Who?" asked Travis.

"I don't know if it's the wolf or if it's Digger. We were closer to him earlier. But there's distance now."

"We aren't going anywhere until the storm lets up." Travis was firm about this. At seventy-one, he wasn't about to risk life and limb, blindly searching for a dog in a blizzard.

"Tomorrow," she said. "There's always tomorrow."

"Tomorrow will be the same as today," said Harriet, her eyes darting furiously at Tom. "What's the future for Sola? What can I promise her? Life is unbearable to her. What is my responsibility? Do I offer her the option of suicide when there's no hope of a cure?"

"Harriet, you can't be serious. Despite her diagnosis, Sola is still a teenager with all the exaggerated emotions of one."

"Could you live with inside voices always taunting you, with a brain constantly sabotaging your perception of reality?"

"We're not Sola. She's still a young woman, learning about herself. She may yet discover strengths in herself that aren't in other people. Think about it. Typically, it's Sola, not Luna, who expresses the compassionate heart. The task for her is to learn to be loving, forgiving, toward herself. When she can do that, then the inner voices will lose their power to keep on hurting her." He caressed the fingertips of Harriet's hand, hoping to soothe her wild grief.

Harriet pulled away. "That's easy for you to say. You work with disabled people. It's bad enough to be imprisoned in a dysfunctional body, but when the mind continually betrays you, nothing in your experience can be trusted. It's not fair, damn it."

Tom sat there quietly, listening.

"I'm sorry," she said. "I don't mean to jump on you, but you can't know how many friends and family members offer well-meaning platitudes with regard to Sola. 'She'll grow out of it.' Or 'You'll have to find a mental institution for her.' She's my daughter. I won't give up on her. I won't."

"Of course, you won't." His voice was soft, gentle, and kind. "But Sola has grown up all along expecting that something would restore her, that some day she could be normal, like everyone else. In most of us, that drive for perfection cracks a nasty whip. We beat ourselves up for our failures as children, as parents, as human beings. When we can acknowledge our limitations, when we can be compassionate toward ourselves, there is no longer a need to flog ourselves with curses and name-calling."

"The inner voices."

"The inner voices in all of us. You've tried to be as good a parent to Sola as possible, but despite all that love, Harriet, you can't heal her. You can't make whole what the Deletion has scrambled."

"But I feel like such a failure." Her eyes brimmed with tears. "I want to help her."

"Sola has to understand that while her brain betrays her, her heart and her capacity to love will remain as incredible strengths within her. She can be mentally ill and know it, acknowledge it, accept it, understand it. She can learn about hallucinations and delusions. When the world goes tipsy on her, she can tell people around her, ask them to steady her, to check out what is real and what is not. It's not the life she wanted or would have chosen but, like all of us bent into our own deformities, she'll find her own satisfactions."

"I wish I could believe that." She snorted a laugh.

"What's so funny?"

"What would it have been like if Luna had been the one with the Deletion Syndrome? She'd have made us all totally miserable. Where is she, anyway? She should have been home by now." Harriet frowned, got up, and peered out the foyer window. The snow was falling hard.

Tom came up behind her and wrapped his arms around her.

She leaned her head back against his chest. "Sometimes, it's hell being a parent."

Luna looked at her watch, then back at Caitlin. "Mom will be worried if I don't get home before dark."

"What part of our argument did you overhear that night?"

"Everything. You were yelling at him."

"I'm sorry about that."

"I can even quote what you said: 'Winston, you've broken your promise to all of us. You've become the monster you hated, the politician sidling up to the pig trough, sucking up all that dirty money.'"

"Did I really say all that?"

"Yes. I started paying close attention then. Nobody had ever called my Dad a pig before. You accused him of taking drug money under the table. At first, I thought you meant that Dad was selling drugs, but that wasn't it, was it?"

Caitlin shook her head.

"It was from the drug companies. I figured that out when he started talking about the pharmacological benefits of the Family Act," said Luna.

"You inherited your Dad's smarts," said Caitlin. "The Act is written in such a way that the drug companies benefit. There's no limit to their profit-taking."

"So they bribed him, didn't they?"

"Yes. The transfer of monies to him weren't registered, because they aren't legal."

"So, why did he do it? He doesn't need the money."

Caitlin shrugged her shoulders. "Why are so many of our politicians corrupt from the little county boards to the U.S. Congress? It always comes down to ego, Luna. If you have a core emptiness inside, no amount of consumption is going to change that. But it's a tempting illusion. Does your Dad know that you eavesdropped?"

"Does my father care?" Luna sounded the sarcastic voice.

"Of course he does. He wants to be a good father."

"How can you say that? He trotted my sister up on that stage in front of all those cameras. He used her. As much as she bugs me, she didn't deserve that from him."

"It's the money talking. He probably rationalizes all the expensive and good things he wants to do for his kids. Once upon a time, I believed in him. I admired him for the courage of his convictions. He took unpopular stances. He defended the rights of those without much of a voice, but power and money are seductive. Maybe he simply got older, more cynical. He got greedy. An old story. It's why I left. I didn't stop loving him: I lost respect for him. When that happens, love begins to seep out at the edges, until finally there's nothing left."

"You didn't do anything about it. You didn't tell anyone." Luna looked her straight in the eye.

"He's a powerful man. It would be so easy for him to insure that I never worked on the Hill again." Caitlin sighed. "I'm a coward, I guess. It was one thing for me to blow up and leave him, but quite another to take that next step."

"I can't do that," said Luna.

"Maybe you're a stronger person than I am."

"No, he's my Dad. I can't walk away from him. I can't look him in the eye and pretend to admire him. It's the way he's treated my sister. It's what he's done to my mother. I don't give a shit about whether he makes a lot of money or not. Miz Stands and Mom's new boyfriend say you've got to know what's important."

"They're right, Luna."

"I want my old Dad back, the one whose heart doesn't have a big hole in it."

Caitlin didn't dare speak the truth of it. The man she had idealized, the father for whom Luna still yearned, may never have existed in the first place.

Beacon Hill had shut down earlier than normal due to the snow storm. Leaning back on his swivel chair, Winston retrieved his telephone messages. One came from Harriet regarding the medical appointment with the pediatric neurologist. He dreaded calling her, not for what she might have to say about Sola, but for her put-upon attitude as the suffering woman. Luckily, their independent incomes were such that they didn't bicker about finances, as was the case with so many divorced parents. His conversations with Harriet always seemed to end with her delineation of his failures as a human being. *It could be worse*, he thought. *I could still be married to her.*

He dialed her number and sat back in his chair, chewing on the edge of his finger and looking out the window. The snow was blanketing downtown Boston, transforming the Boston Commons into a picture postcard. He loved the grand old city, the contradiction between its liberal, academic bent and its conservatism in style.

On the third ring, a male voice answered, "The McWhinnie household."

That jarred Winston into an upright position. "To whom am I talking?"

"Tom."

"I don't know any Tom McWhinnie."

"No. I'm Tom Breslin. Would you like to speak to Harriet?"

"I'm calling for Mrs. McWhinnie." Winston knew he was being trifling and proprietary, but who did this fellow think he was answering the McWhinnie phone?

Harriet picked up the telephone, sounding tired and discouraged. "Winston?"

"Who was that man?" His voice, sharp and disagreeable.

She ignored that question. "I saw the pediatric neurologist. They know what is wrong with Sola."

"Well, that's a good thing. Isn't it?"

"She has a Deletion Syndrome on the twenty-second chromosome."

"I don't understand. Something's absent?" Winston racked his brain about chromosomes.

"Part of her DNA. The missing piece causes the other chromosome to match up incorrectly. It's like a chain reaction."

"So how can we fix her?" Winston had great faith in the Boston medical establishment.

"You're not listening to me. It's a deletion that affects every cell of her body. It can't be corrected. That's why we almost lost her as a baby. If it weren't for all those life-saving procedures, Nature would have taken its course with her."

Winston remembered those sleepless nights when Sola's cleft palate caused the formula to run out her nose, while Baby Luna slept peacefully, fat and happy. The doctors diagnosed Sola as a "failure-to-thrive infant," but that only made Harriet and Winston more determined to nurture their sickly twin to health.

"What now?" *Surely, there must be some course of action.*

"They want to do more tests on her. Apparently this particular Deletion Syndrome has one hundred-and-eighty-five possible symptoms and malfunctions. They also want the two of us to come in for genetic testing."

"Why? Do they think that I caused this problem?"

"It's a simple blood test."

"I'd say it's more likely you, Harriet. Take a look at your mother, your flamboyant aunts."

Harriet let those comments fly by, too tired to joust with him. "The neurologist said that a small group of these children have parents who carried the same deletion in their chromosomes. I don't think that's the case with us. Neither one of us ever showed significant learning disabilities, a hallmark of the syndrome. More likely an act of God at the time of conception."

"I don't believe in God, Harriet. Who would be so cruel as to create such a living hell for a child?"

For once, Harriet was inclined to agree with him.

Expecting a battle with the Missus, the man was pleasantly surprised to discover her interest in the Shetland Sheepdog. "Oooo," she cooed. "We'll get him cleaned up. He's a purebred, a beauty at that. We could get a pretty penny for him. He looks strong enough, once we get the bird shot out of him." She rubbed her hands together. "I'd say he's worth at least four hundred dollars."

"Maybe somebody's looking for him. You know, a lost dog."

"Could be. We'll keep it quiet for now. Finders keepers, I'd say."

She tended to Digger, using the tweezers to pull out the stinging bits of metal. He'd like to have bitten her then, only the man held him down, talking to him. "Don't be going on like that. We'll find you a good home." He eyed his woman, gave her a little pinch on the butt. "Maybe even a wealthy home."

"Go on now," she said, laughing.

TWENTY

During dinner, Agatha spoke not a word about her husband's passage, nor did Travis press her. He regaled her with stories from his forty-three years of marriage and child raising, then quickly summarized the loss of his wife, Dorothy, in an unexpected automobile accident. He didn't dwell on the years since the accident, as all the color and excitement of his former life had drained away. Or that he could not bear to part with his house, too large for one person, because it meant permanently saying goodbye to his dead wife. Every room echoed with the emptiness of her absence. After retirement from the judiciary, he had picked up the banjo. Slowly but surely, the music pulled on him, plucking him back from the drag of a melancholic existence.

And then came Agatha.

Over dinner, their conversation floated like an iceberg, only the tips of their lives on display, the rest wallowing in dark, oceanic shadows. Upon returning to the motel room, they stretched out on their separate beds and watched the news. Agatha retreated into the bathroom for a long period. When she emerged after a shower, her lingerie consisted of a man's large, white shirt and grey, stretch shorts.

Travis patted the side of his bed. "Come over here," he said, turning off the television with the remote control. "It's time you finish telling me what happened to Jesse."

"Tomorrow," she said. "I'll tell you tomorrow."

"No, Agatha. Too long, it's been fermenting in you. If not exposed to air, it will turn into bitterness."

Gingerly, she lay down next to him on the bed.

He primed the pump. "He was in pain from the cancer. He wanted to die."

Agatha closed her eyes and began talking. "The cancer was like a hungry beast eating everything inside him, all his muscle and fat. Jesse shrank into a bony skeleton of his old self. But worst of all, the cancer sucked up all his hope and vision. Some people leave this life in a graceful manner, but not my big man. He grew angry and mean as a tick. Said the Spirits had let him down, that he'd worked hard for the people, and this was how They rewarded him. He turned his back on the Sacred Pipe and the old ways. When the pain got really bad, he cursed me, because I didn't have the knowledge or the wisdom to heal him."

"But he refused to return to the hospital."

Agatha shook her head. "By then, what was the use? The doctors told him to get his affairs in order. It was simply a matter of time, before the cancer killed him. What they offered was sedation, the sleep-before-death."

"Why did he think you could heal him?"

Agatha opened her eyes and looked at him. "Because my grandmother and my aunties had taught me about the plants. There is an old story among the people, that there was a time when the human beings fell out of balance. They didn't hunt with respect. They didn't offer tobacco to the spirits of the animals they killed. So the animals held a council meeting to talk about these human beings. Each animal agreed that if one of them was killed in a careless manner, a Spirit animal would follow the hunter back to his home and give someone in the hunter's family a particular illness. Each animal family developed a different disease. For example, the deer nation would give someone in the hunter's family rheumatism; the fish would bring digestive disorders and so forth. But the plant nation felt sorry for these ignorant human beings. In response, they each cultivated a medicine to match a disease brought by the animal nations. Jesse expected me to discover the herbal medicine to cure his cancer."

"What did you do?" Travis asked.

"I took my Sacred Pipe out and asked the Spirits to help me. They led me to a plant which I collected and steeped into a dark brew. I prayed that They would heal this man I loved." Tears gathered in her eyes and her voice trembled ever so slightly.

Travis wrapped his arm around her. He could feel her tense against the grief.

"I told Jesse that the tea came from the Spirits. He drank it, then fell into a sleep from which he never awoke." The tears crested her eyelids and began to drip down her cheeks. She didn't try to wipe them away.

"Because in our world, Travis, healing doesn't always mean that you get rid of the illness. Sometimes healing comes in the guise of death. A crossing over into the next life."

"And so his friends thought you had poisoned him?"

Agatha nodded.

"Did you know that the tea would kill him?"

Agatha momentarily looked away. "Yes." The tears rolled off her cheeks onto the shirt.

Travis pulled her closer. "It was an act of mercy, Agatha. He was hurting."

"Many times, I've told myself that, but if Jesse had known what would happen, he wouldn't have drunk the tea. He didn't want to die. He raged against the cancer. The truth is that I poisoned him, because I couldn't stand the pain of watching him wither in body and soul. I murdered him." Agatha's whole being shook with inconsolable sobs.

Travis didn't know what else to do but to hold her. Legally, she was right. It was a form of mercy killing but since Jesse hadn't assented to it, it would be considered an act of murder in the eyes of the law. Nor would any court accept the defense of *The Spirits made me do it.*

He stroked her hair as she cried, a grief pent up too long by fear and revulsion.

How quickly he had grown to appreciate this mysterious woman with her paranormal interests and awesome strengths, and now he loved her even more when she was pitiful and in despair. *We human beings are a fragile lot*, he thought. *Oh, Agatha, you don't know how you have restored my heart. I was a walking dead man after Dorothy's accident, and you have brought me back to life. I will do whatever I can to help you.*

Jeffrey dropped Luna off at her house, sorely disappointed in the nothingness of their afternoon drive to Boston.

"Thanks," she said to him.

"Will I see you again?" he asked, silently vowing that he wasn't taking her on any more long, boring trips.

"I'll be around." She grabbed her school books and headed toward the front door.

It wasn't what you'd call much of a promise.

"Where have you been?" asked Harriet, upon Luna's entrance into the house. "I was worried sick. Who was that boy in the car?"

"Just a friend, Mom. Jeffrey Porter."

"I told you that I want to meet all of your friends, before you take off in their cars. Remember?"

"He's not really that much of a friend. If I brought him up to the house to introduce him, he'd think I was sweet on him."

"You spent the whole afternoon with him, Luna. I would say that showed some interest on your part."

"Oh, Mom. You make things so complicated. I don't give a hoot about Jeffrey Porter. It was his car I needed."

Harriet stood there, hands on her hips, wanting answers. Tom entered into the foyer, two sherry glasses in his hand.

"So, where did he take you?" Harriet asked.

Tom handed her a glass of sherry and indicated with his head that he was taking the other glass upstairs to Opal. He gave Harriet a brief, encouraging smile as he left the foyer.

"If you have to know, I went to see Caitlin."

"Why?"

"I had to talk to her about Dad."

"About?"

"Jeez, Mom, why are you cross-examining me like I'm a criminal?"

"For one thing, you've already violated several family rules. You left school without telling me. You got into a car with an unknown male. Then you took a secret trip to Boston. It's like you don't feel any obligation to be a part of this family. What if something had happened to your grandmother, Justin, or Sola? How would I have gotten in touch with you when I hadn't the slightest idea where you were?"

"That's why we need cell phones."

"Don't even go there, Luna. Besides, your cell phone is with Agatha. Now, if it weren't for Tom, I don't know what I would have done with Agatha off chasing after your dog. You're going to have to decide whether you're part of this family or not."

Luna's lower lip began to tremble. Her voice began to rise. "What are you saying, Mom? Are you planning to kick me out?"

"Don't be so dramatic, Luna." Harriet could feel the tidal wave of adolescent hysteria about to come crashing down.

Luna's breath grew choppy; her lower lip stuck way out. "You love Sola better than me, because she's a goody two shoes, Mommy's little baby. You love Justin better because he's the youngest and a boy. Why are you always on my case? I'm human too."

Like a heavy, woolen blanket, fatigue settled onto Harriet's shoulders. She immediately regretted not so much the words, but her tone of voice, hard and dismissive. Little did her daughter realize that the fear of losing her lurked behind Harriet's angry words.

"Why don't you love me like you love them?" wailed Luna, before running out of the room in tears.

Harriet stood there by the front door, sighed, and took a big sip of sherry, wondering how the core sweetness of a mother's love could so easily curdle into edgy splatters of bitter vinegar.

"Opal, I brought you some sherry," Tom announced, as he entered into her bedroom.

"Come in, come in," she said. Opal was busily emptying her bureau drawers and sorting clothes on her bedspread. "I would love to have some sherry. Won't you come sit down?"

"Of course I will. You look like you're getting ready to pack."

She took the glass from him and settled on her couch. "Yes, I'm going away. I don't know where Harriet stashed my suitcase."

Tom raised his eyebrows. *Harriet hadn't said anything about her mother leaving on a trip.*

"It's time for me to go, don't you think? Harriet is so tired. I don't want to become another burden to her."

"Where will you go?"

Opal's brow furrowed. "I don't really know. I thought maybe I could find an apartment. Do you know of one near here? I'd like to be close to Harriet and the grandchildren."

Tom shook his head, trying to think fast on his feet. "I don't think it's a good time for you to leave."

"Oh?"

"You're absolutely right that Harriet is overwhelmed at times, especially about Sola. I think she needs all the support we can give her right now. In fact, I'm sure if you told her you were leaving, she would burst into tears. You're her mother, and she needs you now."

"You really think so?"

Tom nodded vigorously. "I think she would be at a loss without your calming presence." He could hear the rise of angry voices downstairs, especially that of Luna. He stood up.

Opal smiled at him. "Alright. I'll stay as long as she needs me."

Tom bent over and planted a kiss upon the old woman's cheek and hastened down the stairs, passing a furious Luna storming in the opposite direction.

Opal tucked a wisp of white hair behind her ear and smiled. "Thank you for the sherry, Edgar."

"I think it'll be okay to leave him in the house alone. Seems like a civilized dog. We won't be gone long." The woman patted Digger on the head. He was curled up near their wood stove, sleepy from the food and the painful extraction of bird shot. The house door shut before he realized what had happened.

He was alone.

Under stress, Digger resorted to what Digger knew best. He proceeded to attack the door, clawing and splintering the shiny wood. It didn't matter that his body still hurt. When his attempts to get out didn't work, Digger looked around to see what else he could destroy.

TWENTY-ONE

The phone rang. Harriet ran to answer it, but Justin got there first.

"Hello," he said. "My name's Justin. I'm almost six." Then he held out the receiver toward his mother and whispered, "She wants to talk to you."

"Mrs. McWhinnie?" A female voice on the line.

"Yes."

"I'm Lolly Nosrap from the Boston group of—"

"I'm sorry. I don't do donations by the phone," interjected Harriet, about to hang up.

"No," said the woman. "We're not a charity. We're part of a network of VCFS support groups. I got your name from the social worker at the hospital. She said you had expressed interest in hearing from other VCFS parents. Now is Justin the one with the Deletion 22 Syndrome?"

"No," said Harriet. "It's my fifteen-year-old daughter, Sola. What does your group do?"

"Our primary purpose is to give support and to educate family members about caring for a person with Velo-Cardio-Facial Syndrome. There is also the VCFS Educational Foundation that publishes a newsletter, provides a forum for discussion of the problems and treatments of VCFS, and advocates for VCFS patients and their doctors."

"I didn't think there was any treatment," said Harriet.

"There's no cure for it, that's for sure. Some of the particular symptoms, however, can be alleviated or resolved by medicine, surgery, and/or management of the immediate environment. There are VCFS conferences all around the world. The main thing you need to know, Mrs. McWhinnie, is that you're not alone in having to cope with this disorder. Would you like me to send you information about our next meeting?"

"You said your name is Lolly?"

"Yes."

"Then call me Harriet. I sure could use any and all help that's available. It's been so damn lonely going from one doctor to another, trying to find out what's behind all her problems. It would take me several hours just to detail all the different diagnoses, operations, prescriptions, and strange symptoms of my daughter."

"I know how you feel. My son's eleven. He's already undergone five different surgeries."

"I hope you don't mind my posing a personal question?" Harriet held her breath.

"Feel free to ask me anything." Lolly's voice was calm, welcoming, pragmatic.

"Is your son psychotic?"

There was a pause in the conversation. "Not yet. I'm keeping my fingers crossed. Your daughter?"

"When she became an adolescent, she began hearing all sorts of voices. They say it's because her good chromosome has—"

"A low activity gene," interjected Lolly.

"So you know about all that?" asked Harriet.

"I do. It's so hard to watch your own child struggle all the time. You want her to live a normal life. A quirk at conception, a misplaced chromosome. It's not fair, is it?"

"Amen," echoed Harriet.

What a relief, she thought. *Not only do I finally know what is wrong with Sola, but there are others out there in the same boat. I'm no longer paddling up this long, lonely river by myself.*

All night long, Travis slept fitfully with Agatha's head lying heavily upon his shoulder, her body entwined with his. She had cried herself out and then, like a child, had promptly fallen asleep. If he had been a young man, it would have been a frustrating night to linger so close to a woman he loved without making love. But at seventy-one, he had grown past the tyranny of testosterone and was content to wait for Sleeping Beauty to wake up.

No, what kept him awake was the unfamiliar weight of another body on his skeletal frame, the excitement of the days to come, and the poignant memories of the years gone by. Unbidden, the image of his dead wife kept appearing. It was as if she had entered into the darkened room to give her blessing to this new union and to bid him goodbye. With one arm around Agatha, he reached out with the other to touch the shadows in his peripheral vision. He silently chided himself. *Ghosts exist only in our overactive imaginations.*

Still, if he didn't look straight on, he could catch a glimpse of wife's profile. The way her chin used to set as she concentrated on the task before her, the way the corners of her mouth used to crinkle into a smile.

The fingers of his free hand moved in a slight gesture, waving goodbye to her. Slowly the image fragmented into the dark air, dissipated into moving, tiny, bright dots. Then nothing.

"I love you, Dorothy," he whispered, surprised at the swell of old emotions.

Shifting position, so that Agatha's head now rested on his chest, Travis began to stroke her hair.

She snored ever so lightly.

"I love you, Agatha," he whispered.

When the man and woman returned to their cabin, they couldn't believe their eyes. The door was scratched from mid-level down. Overturned waste paper baskets, their contents strewn over the floors, paper shredded into little bits. It was as if a whirlwind had cycled through the house interior, leaving the walls intact. On their bed, neatly deposited upon the woman's antique quilt, lay a string of turds and a chewed glass thermometer.

"What the . . ?" asked the man, left speechless to describe the devastation.

Standing there beside the bed, the little tornado wagged his tail, relieved to see that the human beings had returned.

"That goddam dog," swore the man, his cheeks flushing crimson with rage. "I'm gonna kill him." He stepped forward to grab the dog.

Digger's ears flattened with the angry tone of voice. He backed up a few steps, scouted his route of escape. The woman entered the room, unknowingly providing a diversion. Digger flashed by the man, slammed into the woman's knees, toppling her, and scooted into the other part of the house.

A commotion followed as the man helped the woman to her feet. "Are you hurt?"

Digger looked around. No exit. He squeezed behind the couch.

The man thundered into the living room. "Where are you, Dog? This is the thanks we get for rescuing you, for cleaning you up? You're gonna wish you'd starved when I get finished with you." The man stumbled about, probing dark corners. He whistled, he grunted, he called the dog all sorts of names.

Digger flattened himself against the wall and made not a sound.

The woman limped into the room. "Leave off, I say. We'll find him soon enough. What were you planning to do to him?"

"Kill him," said the man.

"That's really smart. What use is he to us dead? There's no money in it."

"I'll teach him a thing or two about wrecking our home."

"Sell him."

The man shook his head. "Nah, it'll take too long to find a buyer. By that time, there won't be any house left."

"What about the townie who buys dogs for medical research?"

The man paused in his search and destroy mission and rubbed his chin.

"He'd give at least twenty dollars for the dog. Think about it," she continued. It wasn't much but it was better than nothing.

He peered behind the couch. "Aha, there you are, skulking like a goddam coward. Well, you're mine now." He reached down to grab Digger by the ruff.

And that is when Digger bit him hard on the hand.

"Why are you crying?" asked Justin. "Did you fall down?"

"I don't want to live anymore." Sola looked up from her bed, where she had been sobbing into a pillow.

"Why?"

"Because I can't be fixed. Because I'm the bad twin and Luna is the good twin. Because God must hate me."

"I don't hate you."

"You're not God." Sola tried to keep her voice angry and sullen. She wanted God to know that she would never, ever forgive Him.

"And I love you more than I do Luna."

Now that softened Sola's heart. She held out her hand to her little brother. "Why do you love me more?"

"Because."

"Because what?"

"Because you don't push me away."

Sola smiled and pulled her brother closer, enveloping him in a full body hug.

Even though he felt smothered, Justin sensed that his sister needed to hold onto him. He stood there and took it like a man. His face pressed against her stomach, his voice muffled, he announced, "I'm going to be a doctor someday and make you all well."

After breakfast, Tom arrived to watch Opal. The kids had already scattered to school. Harriet gathered up her purse, her keys, her portfolio bag and was about to head out the door. Tom walked her out to the car. The sun was shining and bright, already melting the last blast of winter.

"It's too beautiful a day to go to work, Harriet. The crocuses are coming up through the snow, the trees are budding, the birds are building nests and chirping love songs. Are you sure you can't stay home on such a glorious day?"

"You're certainly chipper this morning. Must have been the coffee," she said, opening the driver's door.

"Not the coffee," he said. "Good news."

"Oh?"

"My brother, Leon, called last night, left a message for me to get in contact with him. Seems like he's rediscovered his need for family. He wants us to get together."

"When will you see him?"

"Tonight. He's been real depressed about Dad, about our situation. I think he's ready to heal the breech between us. I certainly hope so. We've always been close, and this thing with Dad has torn us apart."

"How can you forgive him for all those angry words in that newspaper interview, calling you a 'despicable traitor,' and that he wished you 'dead and gone to hell.' Are you sure he's not going to greet you with a gun and shoot you? I don't know if I'd have the ability to reconcile with someone like that." Harriet slammed shut the car door, then lowered the window.

Tom leaned through the window and gave her a peck upon the cheek. "No family is perfect. He's my brother. He's had to sort through a lot of garbage to forgive me. He must know now that I still love Dad."

"You're not the one who needs forgiveness," Harriet said.

"We all need to be forgiven, Harriet. None of us live perfect lives." He smiled. "Except for you, of course." He reached in through the car window and stroked her cheek.

Amused, she chuckled. He had a way of making her laugh with his absurd tags at the end of profound statements. Backing the car out of the driveway, she waved to him before speeding off to work. The ocean sun glinted brilliantly off the car's hood, the sky blue and cloudless, the air crisp with promise, the ground turning to slush with Spring warmth. He was right about the day.

TWENTY-TWO

"The dog's dead meat," exclaimed the man, as his wife bandaged his hand. "No one's gonna want a vicious animal like him. You get me a rope. I'll cinch it to his neck, throw it over a branch, I will."

The woman slapped his bitten hand.

"Hey, that hurts," he yelled. He glared at her, then stopped, recognizing that fierce look in her eyes, the rigid set to her jaw. Her mind was made up.

"I'm going to take that dog and sell it and don't you get in my way," she said. "Maybe twenty dollars isn't much to you, but it sure is to me."

He looked away from her intensity. She could be really scary at times like these.

"Go call that guy who buys dogs," she ordered. "Tell him we got one for him, to come right now before you do anything foolish."

The woman unplugged an extension cord, then extracted a piece of baloney from the refrigerator. "Come here, Sweetpea," she cooed to Digger. "I've got a treat for you."

Slowly but surely, the piece of baloney, the smell of it, the sight of it, lured Digger out from behind the couch. She pulled off a section of meat and palmed it to him. He gobbled it up and wagged his tail to show he meant her no harm and could she give him some more, please? He edged closer.

She placed the baloney on the floor and her arm around his neck, tying the cord for a temporary leash. "That a boy," she said. "You're not so scary, after all."

He looked up, swishing his tail back and forth. Meanwhile from the other room, the man spoke into the telephone. Digger kept a wary eye in that direction.

"He's not so bad," said the woman. "Quick to anger though. It's all a big bluff, you know. Lots of hollering and thrashing about. Men don't want you to know when fear's gripped their bowels."

The man returned, surprised to see a docile dog standing leashed by his wife. "Just leave him be," she cautioned.

"Bobby'll be up here in the hour," he replied, pretending that he had neither heard her last order nor noticed the dog.

Before long, a white, windowless van pulled up by the house. A man with a dirty beard and long, stringy hair jumped out and unlocked the back, revealing two rows of stacked wire cages. In the bottom crates clamored three beagles, two terrier mixes, and a very pregnant spaniel. He opened the door to one crate and headed toward the house, just as the woman walked out with Digger on her makeshift leash.

"Hiya, Bobby, how you doing?"

Bobby whistled. "That's a purebred Shetland Sheepdog. Don't see too many of them. Your man sure got his dander up."

The woman laughed. "You know how he is. So, what will you give me for this dog?"

"Ten dollars."

"C'mon, Bobby, you yourself said he was a purebred. I'd say thirty be about right."

"Twenty then."

"Done." She handed him the leash.

Digger looked with interest at the other dogs, nose in the air, trying to figure out where they came from, where they were going.

Bobby scooped him up, shoved him into the wire crate, and secured the latch. He dug into his pocket for the cash. "Where's your husband?"

"He don't want you to see his bandaged hand. The dog bit him."

"This little guy?" Bobby stuck his fingers into the wire crate. Digger wagged his tail on cue and licked his hand. "He's a lover, not a fighter. Like me." He winked at her before slamming shut the van's back door.

"Go on now," she replied, giving him a playful shove on the arm.

"You sure he didn't steal this dog from somebody's lawn?" asked Bobby, heading around to the driver's side.

The woman frowned.

"Not that I care one way or the other," Bobby continued. "I'm just supposed to ask." He climbed into the van. "But if you find any more dogs, call me, and I'll come get 'em."

He backed the van and hauled the load down the old country road thinking, *It's a good business. Hell, these dogs would probably be euthanized at a pound anyway. This way, they get to live a few months more in some medical laboratory.* He bought them at ten dollars a head and sold them for about hundred a head. Not a bad profit, as long as he didn't let himself look too deeply into their fearful eyes.

A man's gotta do what a man's gotta do to earn a living, he told himself. *They're just dogs, after all. Not my fault that God saw fit to put us at the top of the food chain.*

In the morning, Agatha awakened suddenly with a sharp stab of anxiety. She untangled herself from the arms of a sleeping Travis and slipped out of bed. Peering out the motel window, a clear Maine morning greeted her with only a few, sea-bent clouds scudding across the sky. From her duffel bag, she extracted a wolf skin and her medicine bundle wrapped in an Indian baby blanket, tied with two leather cords. Kneeling down on the wolf skin, she opened the bundle.

Inside lay several objects: stones, feathers, an ear of dried corn, Indian sage, cedar, a packaged mix of tobacco and herbs, a pipe bag, a turtle shell, and other items particular to her spiritual medicines. She rolled a few sprigs of the sage into a ball, placed it in the turtle shell, and then lit it. In the smoke of the sage, Agatha cleansed herself, the contents of her bundle and, for good measure, the rest of the motel room, including Travis. His nose wrinkled, but he simply sighed and kept on sleeping.

Agatha assembled the red stone pipe bowl to the stem, offering it to the Grandfather Sky and then to the Grandmother

Earth. With little pinches of the sacred tobacco, dipped in the smudge of the sage, she made prayers to Waken Tanka, the Sacred Mystery, then to the Grandfathers, the Grandmothers in All the Directions, to Grandfather Sky, Grandmother Earth, and to the spotted eagle, Wanbli Gleska. Holding the Pipe with the bowl toward her heart and the stem toward the West, she prayed, "Tunkasila, Grandfather, I ask Your help in finding the lost dog. He is important to the McWhinnie family, to me. Digger's been teaching the young woman, Luna, what it means to be a human being. She needs that healing. I call upon my medicine, the wolf, to find him, lead us to him. Mitakuye Oyas'in. All my relations."

Still Travis slept on, despite the prayers and the smoke of the smoldering sage. That is, until Agatha let loose with the mournful howl of a wolf.

Travis shot up in bed, his eyes frantically scanning the room for the wild animal. *Where's Agatha? There, down on the floor. By God, the sound of the wolf is coming from her!* His heart thumping, he grabbed his glasses from the bed stand, fearful that he might discover his newly beloved having sprouted fur and fangs, but no, Agatha was holding a long Indian pipe. Although she had retained her human form, her eyes had gone glassy, unfocused. He kept still so as not to distract her.

She was murmuring, yipping, then quietly nodding her head, as if in conversation with someone else. He looked round the room but nobody else was there. Since he knew he couldn't go back to sleep, he sat there against the pillows, quietly watching her do a Pipe ceremony.

When she completed her prayers, she lit the tobacco in the bowl, offered the Pipe to All the Directions, then smoked in silence. Upon finishing, she struggled to her feet, cracked open the motel door, and blew out the bowl's ashes, saying, "Mitakuye Oyas'in."

She shut the door, placed the bowl and stem back in her pipe bag, wrapped and tied her bundle, rolled up the wolf skin, and inserted them back into her duffel bag.

Only then did she acknowledge his presence. "Good morning, Travis. Did I wake you up?"

"That was as realistic a wolf sound as I've ever heard from a human being. You're human, aren't you? I'd hate to have fallen in love with a vampire."

She was smiling. "Time's running out on us. We've to head further west. Let's grab some coffee to go."

He angled out of bed and rubbed his eyes. "Do you do this every morning?"

"Do what?"

"Wake the dead with a lupine howl?"

"Thank you," she said. "for letting me talk last night."

"For letting you fall asleep in my arms," he added.

"That too." She smiled. "It wasn't all that romantic, was it?"

He got to his feet and stretched. "Well, I think one wolf in this relationship is quite enough."

Winston searched the Internet. The name of Tom Breslin had struck a familiar chord. Bingo, his computer quickly zeroed in on the newspaper stories of the two brothers and the killer father. He picked up the telephone and dialed Harriet's work number.

"Hello, may I help you?" Harriet was in full professional voice.

"It's me," Winston said.

"What do you want?" she asked.

"I see you've got a new boyfriend."

"Winston, that's my private life. Now, unless you have something to communicate to me about the kids, I don't see this as any business of yours."

"But it is about the kids, Harriet. First, you hire a nanny of unknown origin to watch over our kids, and now you're exposing them to a man from a homicidal family. If I might say so, it reflects an appalling lack of judgement on your part."

"Get off my back, Winston. I don't have to listen to your belittling comments anymore." She promptly hung up.

Winston sat there in his office, the sound of disconnection beeping and scolding him through the phone receiver. He drummed his fingers on his desk, thinking. There was a time when he could make Harriet beam with radiant joy at his compliments or reduce her to instant tears with his criticisms, a time when he knew that what he valued or didn't value was important to her. But that was no longer true. She acted as if she didn't care one way or the other.

His knuckles began rapping on the desk. Nobody, but nobody, hung up on him without there being consequences.

At the school cafeteria, the four adolescent girls soon grew tired of talking about the boys and started comparing parents. Luna's best friend, Judy, the one with the flawless skin, the silky hair, the spotless face, and a straight A average spoke up first. "When I was in elementary school, Mother told me if I brought home anything less than an A, they were going to ship me off to reform school."

"No," exclaimed the others.

"What's worse was that I totally believed her."

"That's cruel," said Anna.

"But you're still getting As," protested Luna.

Judy blushed. "I guess it's become a habit. That's why I like going to your house. Your Mom's so cool. If you brought home a B, she wouldn't rag on you."

"She doesn't even know I exist," complained Luna. "Except when she needs me to babysit my brother, my twin sister, or my grandmother. Sometimes our house is like an insane asylum."

"I like your kid brother. He's cute. Your grandmother seems sweet to me," said Judy.

"She's okay."

"What's with your sister?" asked Carol. "You two are so different."

"She's got something wrong with her chromosomes. It can't be fixed. When she was born, there were a lot of things wrong in her body."

"Is she retarded?"

Luna shook her head. "No. She's got learning disabilities, cerebral palsy, but she reads a lot, mainly biographies of famous, beautiful people."

"Stories of perfect people leading perfect lives," added Judy.

"So, you came out of the womb okay and she didn't," said Anna. "That's really freaky."

"Twin chromosomes. Twin girls. Neither set matches," said Judy. "But your Mom seems to have coped okay. What about your Dad?"

"I don't want to talk about him," replied Luna.

"Ooo, that's a sore spot," said Anna. "I thought you were his favorite."

Luna began stuffing potato chips into her mouth, one right after another. It didn't help. She drained a can of soda. The glob of chewed chips slogged slowly down her throat into her stomach. She felt bloated and queasy.

"I wish Sola had never been born," said Luna. "My Dad left because of her."

"No," said the others.

"Mom spends much more time with her than with me. Even today, she's leaving work early to take Sola to the doctors for some appointment. So, of course, I can't hang out with you this afternoon. I have to march straight home from school to babysit my brother and grandmother. The person who's watching them in the morning has to go to work. It's not fair."

They all nodded in sympathy.

Luna excused herself and headed to the girls' bathroom before afternoon classes. Her stomach hurt. She entered a stall and closed the door. It would be so easy to thrust two fingers down her throat and get rid of the discomfort. She thought about Agatha and her promise.

The bathroom door opened and in walked Judy.

"Luna, is that you?" she asked, peering under the stall door.

"Yes. You don't happen to have a cigarette?" Luna sat down on the toilet and, feeling dizzy, lowered her head.

"Not here." Judy entered into the next stall and closed the door. "Besides, we'd get caught for sure. You okay?"

"No. I hurt."

There was quiet for a moment, except for the tinkle of piss and the snap of toilet paper off the rack.

"I'd hurt too, if Sola was my sister," Judy said.

"You would?"

"I wouldn't know how to reconcile the guilt of being the healthy one with the struggles of my sister. I'd have to pretend I didn't care, you know, harden myself so that no one would know how I really felt." Judy stood up, assembled her clothes, and kicked the flusher. She opened the stall door and washed her hands in the sink.

Luna remained seated on the toilet.

"Are you coming?" asked Judy.

"In a minute. Go on," said Luna. She could hear the bathroom door swish shut.

She stood up and leaned against the stall door. Maybe Judy was right. Maybe all her anger at Sola and at her mother was because she couldn't tolerate her own guilt.

She opened the door and walked to the sink, the urge to vomit having temporarily vanished. Running the cold water, she splashed her face with it, then examined her mirrored reflection.

Have I been lying to myself all this time?

Accusing eyes looked back at her, demanding the truth.

Harriet scrambled from work to pick up Sola and ferry her to yet another doctor's appointment. This time, it was for an MRI of the brain.

"Is it going to hurt?" asked Sola.

The technicians reassured her that it wouldn't. She would have to remain still for about thirty minutes in a long cylinder in which magnetic resonating images would be taken of her brain tissue.

"I have VCFS," Sola informed the female technician.

The technician secured her head, so that Sola wouldn't move. "Your mother brought in one of your favorite pieces of music, Brahms' Deutsche Requiem. Would you like us to play it for you over the speakers?"

"Yes," answered Sola, her eyes wide with fright.

"I'm looking forward to hearing it for the first time. I'll be in the next room, handling the controls." The technician was trying to make conversation as she settled the girl into the machine.

Distracted, Sola said, "When I listen to it, I think of God."

"Wow," said the technician. "It's that powerful, huh?"

"It makes me cry. I think it makes God cry. There's all that dark storm in the music, and then, it's like the sun bursts though into the most beautiful harmonies. It's like a promise that things will get better."

"Incredible." The technician patted her hand, before leaving the room. "Are you ready?"

An hour later, the radiologist asked to see Harriet in his office. Up on the lit board were the various views of Sola's brain. "Fascinating," he said. With a pointer, he zeroed in on the surface of the cerebral hemispheres. "As you can see, there is a difference in the two hemispheres of her brain. This one shows an unusually large number of small fissures, in comparison with the other one. Also, notice the enlarged ventricles, which we are seeing in other VCFS patients."

"What does all this mean?" asked Harriet.

The physician shrugged his shoulders. "At this point, we don't know. The brain is enormously complex. There are definitely anatomical differences between the normal brain and those of Deletion 22 individuals. We're at the point of describing the differences, but we're not far enough along in our knowledge to say what specifically causes certain symptoms."

He took down the MRI images. "The visual-spatial tests on Sola revealed such severe perceptual problems that we don't know how your daughter was ever able to learn to read. She has severe dyslexia. Yet, the psychologist tells me that she's above average in her verbal skills." He shook his head in amazement. "It's incredible how the brain learns to adapt, isn't it?"

Somehow, Harriet couldn't summon up an enthusiastic response.

"They tell me that she has psychotic episodes," he continued. Harriet nodded.

"We suspect that her brain is mixing up the signals and feeding her false information." He then bombarded Harriet with the description of various neurotransmitter actions and cerebral locations that displayed incontrovertible evidence of the deep faults that quaked throughout the whole of Sola's brain.

On poor shocks, the white van sloshed and skidded on the melting road surfaces as Bobby drove southeast, heading toward Boston and its medical facilities. He wanted to be done with the day's run in time to head back up north. He stopped along the way to pick up some more dogs, until the van was full of the yammering and yipping canines. Luckily, Bobby had brought along ear phones and his portable CD player to out-blast the noise.

Seven miles away, Travis and Agatha were driving northwest, on the same country road that would intersect with the white van.

Travis didn't share his fears about this being a wild goose chase. *Time with Agatha is time well spent,* he reasoned. But he doubted that they'd ever find the lost dog.

Agatha turned off the car radio, all the better to listen to what the natural and supernatural world had to tell her. She sensed that they were close, that if they missed this opportunity, they'd never find Digger. He'd be gone forever. She kept her eyes open, scanning for any sign of him in the landscape speeding by.

A red tailed hawk fluttered down on top of a telephone pole. Nothing unusual there. It was watching the road for any accidental kill that might come its way. The sun glinted off its wings.

The clouds of morning had been replaced by a deep, peaceful blue sky. In this time of seasonal change, the hard wood branches reached out toward the sun with red-tipped fingers. The unencumbered Maine pines stood like sentinels, straight and stalwart, bending only slightly in the breeze. The car passed shadows shifting on the ground. Agatha noted these observations and waited for something else.

A few automobiles sped by: one red sedan, two black pickup trucks, four SUVs, and one white van. Nothing unusual, except for a subtle shift inside of her. Whereas before she had felt taut, expectant, forward, now it was like a band being stretched thinner and thinner, a connection about to snap.

Bobby sang loudly and off-key to the lonely country tune in his ear phones. His van spewed melted slush on the passing cars as he sped toward Boston, the jerkiness of the ride rattling the crates in the back.

For a fraction of a moment, he saw a dark blur running alongside the edge of the road. *A large dog*, he thought. *Another hundred dollars.* But before he could slow down, the animal veered in front of the van. Bobby hit the brake. The van skidded off the road, out of control. Bobby frantically spun the steering wheel in the opposite direction. The van careened up an embankment, following the logic of speed and ice, then rolled over and over down into a ditch. Glass splattered and metal crumbled, until the van settled upside down, its wheels still spinning.

In the violent tumble, the back door had popped open, and some crates had spilled out, dogs and all. A few cage latches had broken, its occupants scattering toward freedom. Trapped in the smoking wreckage, Digger was not among them.

Lifeless, Bobby dangled upside down, strapped into his seat belt, his neck broken, with the ear phones still singing a melancholy tune of broken hearts and misplaced love.

TWENTY-THREE

"Go back, go back," ordered Agatha.

"What?"

"I said go back. Turn around. Now."

Travis slowed the car down and did a U turn. He wondered if Agatha had finally given up, resigning herself to the disappearance of Digger. "Are we going home now?"

Agatha let down the car window. "We're almost there."

Travis looked around. "'There is no there there,'" he said.

Agatha looked at him.

"It was something that Gertrude Stein said when she returned home to Oakland, California, but home had changed. We're retracing our steps. Are we headed back home?"

"Not without Digger," she said. "Over there." She pointed. "Slow down now. Pull over."

He did as he was told.

Three dogs were milling by the side of the road, as if waiting for human direction. A wisp of smoke spiraled over the side embankment. Agatha jumped out of the car and charged up the hill. At the top, she frantically waved for Travis to follow.

Upside down in a ditch rested the crumpled remains of the smoking white van, dog crates scattered on the ground every which way. Passing her, three dogs charged down the slope, barking at the back of the van.

Travis caught up to her and signaled for her to stand back, lest the van ignite and explode. Agatha paid him no mind. "Check the driver," she ordered. "I'll see to the rear." She scrambled down the hill, past the crates to the van's back door. Several dogs were still locked in their cages. She unlatched them, one by one, liberating the animals.

"The driver's dead!" yelled Travis. "I'll call the police on my cell phone. Be careful, Agatha." He retreated up the hill to retrieve a phone signal.

Everything was a mess in the back of the van, tossed topsy turvy. It looked as if the wire cages were all empty. Reaching way back inside of the van, she pulled one last crate forward.

And there was Digger, fiercely wagging his tail and barking at her.

When she wrenched open the cage door, he jumped into her arms with such force that it propelled her backwards, both of them falling to the ground. Digger covered her face with doggie kisses, as she rolled awkwardly to her feet.

"Down, Digger," she ordered.

He immediately dropped to the down position, quivering with joy.

Agatha noticed the bloody patches on his skin. "What happened to you? You look as if someone peppered you with buckshot."

Travis came up to them. "I've never seen him so obedient," he said. "The police will be here any minute now with an ambulance. I also told them to contact the Humane Society, that there is a passel of dogs here needing homes."

"But not this one," said Agatha, leaning over and stroking the ears of the panting Sheltie, while continuing to puzzle over his wounds. "This one's coming back home with us."

Digger's tail thumped the ground in total agreement.

"They found him! They found him!" screamed Luna, hanging up the phone and running throughout the house.

"Edgar?" asked Opal, looking up from her book on the lost continent of Atlantis.

"No, Grandma. They found Digger. My dog."

"Your father's dog."

"No. My dog," asserted Luna. "He became my dog when we started running agility courses."

Justin ran up the stairs from the basement television room to find out why Luna was yelling.

"They found Digger!" Luna picked up her brother and twirled him about, much to his delight. She planted a big, sloppy kiss on his cheek which he promptly palmed off, then lowered him to the ground. "You know what? I'm going to go into the kitchen and cook dinner, have it all ready for Mom and Sola when they get home from the doctors."

"What about Agatha?" asked Opal.

"She'll arrive later with Travis and Digger," answered Luna. "C'mon Justin, do you want to cook dinner with me? It'll be fun."

Slowly but surely, Justin shook his head. He didn't trust this sudden burst of enthusiasm from his mercurial sister. She had the ability to drop from glee to glum in a nanosecond. It was safer to watch television.

Harriet was pleasantly surprised by the hot meal awaiting them when she and Sola entered the house. The sweet smell of barbecued beef simmering on top of the stove made their mouths water. The table was neatly set with ice in the glasses, salad in the center bowl, sliced bread on the cutting board, and two sherry glasses on the kitchen counter. Luna greeted them from the kitchen doorway.

"Agatha must have come back," said Harriet, shucking off her coat.

"Nope," answered Luna, grinning.

Harriet helped Sola out of her jacket. "I thought Tom had to go to work this afternoon and evening."

"He did," said Luna.

Harriet turned and noticed her mother in the living room, sound asleep over a book. "Well, then who cooked supper?"

Luna performed a theatrical bow.

Harriet raised her eyebrows. "You?"

"I know how to cook."

"I'm stunned," said her mother. "To what do we owe this honor?"

Luna move forward and picked up her mother's hand and also Sola's hand. "They found him."

"Digger?" screeched Sola.

"Yes."

The two teenagers began to jump up and down with joy, hugging each other and laughing.

Harriet's mouth dropped open. "It's a miracle," she said. *But I don't believe in miracles*, she thought.

After a dinner hour filled with speculation about Agatha's retrieval of Digger, the telephone rang. Luna ran to answer it.

"Hi, Luna."

"Tom, we found Digger. Isn't that cool? They're bringing him home tonight."

"Is your Mom right there?" It was unlike him to be so brusque. Luna walked the phone over to her mother, who was loading the dishwasher. She angled off to the side, eavesdropping on the one-sided conversation.

"You heard the news, Tom? Isn't it wonderful? Are you coming over later? Okay. How about tomorrow?"

Luna saw her mother's face morph from a puzzled look to a clouded frown. Something wasn't right. The teenager busied herself with wiping down the dinner table while keeping her ear sharply attuned.

"I don't understand. I know that it's been asking a lot of you to come over and babysit, but that's done now. Agatha's returning tonight," said Harriet, her face wrinkling with concern.

"A time apart? But why now? There's something you're not telling me, Tom. What is it?" Harriet gestured to Luna to leave the kitchen and give her privacy.

Luna edged into the foyer without fully shutting the swinging wooden door. She leaned against the connecting wall.

"No, it's not okay. You can't come plowing into our hearts and then suddenly announce you need a break from us. Tom, I thought we had a terrific relationship. I deserve a better explanation from you, something that would make sense. Can't we meet for coffee later tonight? Well, when?" Constricted, Harriet's voice rose higher in tone.

Luna overheard her mother drop the phone onto the kitchen counter followed by a long moan that cascaded into a liquid sobbing. She snatched a box of tissues and reentered the kitchen. Her mother had slumped to the kitchen floor, knees curled up in front of her, her face covered by two hands. Luna didn't know what to say. She sat down by her weeping mother and silently handed her tissue after tissue.

"Why is my daughter so sad?" asked Opal, hunched over a wooden jigsaw puzzle. "When she gets quiet like this, I know something bad has happened."

"Luna says Tom broke up with her," answered Sola, who had previously claimed the human beings in the picture puzzle but now wished that she had possessed the setting sun, the blue sky, the red, orange, yellow clouds, and the dark green treetops. People were harder to assemble, more complex, than the natural world.

"Hand me those edges there." Opal pointed to a pile of wooden pieces. "When you can build the structure of a thing, then it's much easier to fill in the blank spots. A puzzle will sometimes distract you with all its colors, but when you pay attention to the shape of things, you can see how it all fits together."

"But I like the colors, Grandma, especially blue. They say that is the color of peace and calm." Sola tried unsuccessfully to align two pieces to the main framework of the puzzle.

"When I fell in love with Edgar," said Opal, "the world's mirror glowed with a brilliant light, containing all the precious colors of the rainbow. The yellow sun melted into gold, the grey dew glistened into a burnished silver, the sunset swirled with amber and ruby lines, and night sparkled with diamond stars. Love lifts you out of the ordinary. When it breaks, the glass shatters, the colors dim, and shadows creep across the landscape of your heart. That's what happened when Edgar died."

Sola tried to pound a piece into a place it would not go.

"I tell you, Sola, it's the shape of a life, not its momentary colors, that will finally tell the story."

"Do you think Mom will get back together with Tom? I like him. He's a nice man." Sola found the missing section to the woman under the parasol in the picture. With great satisfaction, she inserted the missing piece. "There, she's complete. She's perfect."

A job well done. Winston smiled. He hadn't lost his touch for making the right move at the right time.

Harriet is mistaken if she thinks she can simply walk out of my life into that of another man. Our lives will always run on the same track, no matter how many derailments there are. We have history, we have memory, we have children; they will always bind us together.

It was, of course, a paradox.

He didn't want to be married to her. Motherhood had aged Harriet beyond the prime of beauty. In her forties, she had become shrill, restive, and too darn independent. There were younger, more attractive women who were flattered by his attentions. No, he had no interest in retracing the old journey.

But he'd be damned if he was simply going to sit on the sidelines while someone else came roaring down the track.

TWENTY-FOUR

"Will you marry me?" Travis asked, keeping his eyes straight ahead, his hands steady upon the wheel of the car.

There was a long pause, a heavy breathing into his right ear. He turned, thinking that Agatha might be whispering something, only to encounter the long nose of Digger inserting himself between the two of them, his front feet on Travis' armrest, his hind feet straddling the back seat.

"Phew, you stink," Travis exclaimed.

"Excuse me?" said Agatha. "Did I hear you right?"

"I was talking about Digger, not you."

"You were proposing marriage to the dog? You white people have a strange set of priorities. He does seem to take a liking to you though."

"Agatha, be serious. Will you marry me?" He was not about to be denied an answer.

She looked out at the passing night scenery. "No," she finally said.

His shoulders sagged. "We could have a lot of fun together. I'm a young seventy-one year old with a lot of life left in me."

"Of that I have no doubt," she said.

"Then why not take a chance? You know I love you. I think you have similar feelings that way too. Or am I just an old coot dabbling in a romantic fantasy?"

"Travis, you're one of the loveliest men I've ever known. I'm honored by your proposal."

"But?"

"When I married Jesse, we did it in the traditional way. We got married by the Chanunpa Wakan, the Sacred Pipe. It means that we'll be together forever: this life, the next, and the one after that."

"I'm not asking you forever. Simply for the remainder of our lives."

"I cannot marry you," she said.

There was a finality to that statement which he could not breech. They drove along in silence for a few more moments.

"Isn't there more that you want to say?" she asked.

"I'm trying to respect your decision."

At that moment, Digger slurped his tongue across Travis' ear. Agatha laughed. "We can't help but love you, Travis."

Some consolation, he thought. *A dog's kiss*. Then it hit him. Agatha had just acknowledged that she loved him.

"If you won't marry me," he spoke haltingly, picking his words carefully, "Will you live with me until the end of our days?"

Agatha turned and smiled. "God, Travis, I thought you'd never get around to asking."

As if to seal the agreement, Digger immediately slobbered kisses on both of them. To Travis, it was a piece of canine folly. Agatha, however, knew that her wolf medicine had returned home to her.

Caitlin punched the security codes. Thank heavens, she still had her security identification badge and that the guard didn't look too closely at the expiration date. She slipped into Winston's office, not bothering to flick on the lights. She didn't want to attract any undue attention.

It didn't take her long to find what she was looking for: the hidden key to the file cabinet, a list of names, recorded donations, and off-shore bank statements. She placed the items upon the copier and fired off two separate copies of each page, one for herself and one for reserve. Her insurance policy if Winston decided to enact revenge upon her for spilling the beans to Luna.

She timed herself, restoring the items to their respective files, locking the cabinet, and returning the key to its hidden storage. Peering out the door to make sure that no one was walking in the hallway, she eased out of Winston's office.

"Good night," she said to the guard at the entrance.

"Have a good one," he answered.

"I will," she promised. *Mission accomplished.*

"It's wrong," Leon protested. "I had no right to ask you to do this." He watched his brother tuck away the cell phone and order another beer. Between them sat the half-eaten remains of their pub food.

"What's done is done," said Tom. "We're family."

"That's what Dad used to say. Remember?"

"I'm not here to fight with you or open those wounds again. You asked me to meet you here. You needed a favor."

"I'm sorry." Leon held up his hand to show he meant no harm. "I'm a lot like him, you know. When that bastard called and threatened to get me kicked off the force, I wanted to kill him. You're the social worker. You think that cops and murderers are mirror images of each other?"

"When you spend all your time trying to chase criminals, you begin to think like them."

Leon chewed the inside of his cheek, sipped his beer in a thoughtful manner. "I could do it in a way that nobody would find out."

Tom shook his head. "Killing doesn't solve anything."

"It'd be easy enough. I could make it look like an accident. Look at you. Depressed as shit, looking like a lonely old toad. It isn't right."

"He's the father of her children. I won't see her again. There'll be no blood shed on my account."

"I don't like asking favors of you," continued Leon, "but being a police officer is the only thing that's holding me together these days. And that bastard has the power to get me fired."

"What is done, is done, Leon." Inside, Tom pushed down the heat of hate rising within him—for Winston, for his father, for his pathetic brother, and for himself.

What kind of man, out of fear, surrenders his one chance for real love?

When Agatha, Travis, and Digger arrived home late that night, the house exploded with joyful reunions. Digger moaned and groaned and rubbed up against everyone, wagging his tail, and sniffing around to make sure that no one had usurped his place in the pack. Everyone lavished sympathy over his mottled fur and bloody scabs.

Only Harriet remained strangely quiet, subdued. Red eyes, flushed cheeks, and the tracks of dried tears informed Agatha that something disturbing had happened. Thinking that it had to do with Sola, Agatha waited until after Travis had departed and the others had trailed off to their own bedrooms.

"I'm relieved you're back, Agatha," said Harriet in a dead voice while scooping up Justin's toys from the floor. "We've exhausted our welcome with Tom."

"Is Sola okay?"

"Temporarily, but we'll continue to lurch from one medical crisis to another with her. At least, we have a name, Velo-Cardio-Facial Syndrome, for what's wrong with her. I'm going to a meeting of VCFS parents in a couple of days."

"What about Justin?"

"He's fine."

"Grandmother?"

Harriet shrugged her shoulders, then answered. "I asked her tonight to tell us once more the story of Ariadne and the magic ball of thread. She mixed up all the names and got lost in the narrative. She couldn't find her way to the story's end. That's going to happen more and more."

"Did she mention anything about nursing homes?"

"That's not going to happen. I know she worries about being a burden to me, but I need her here with me. Does that strike you as odd, Agatha?"

"There will come a time when she won't be able to tell you what she really wants."

"I know. But it's non-negotiable. She stays as long as we can physically handle the challenge of caring for her."

To Agatha's reckoning, that left the other twin as the problem. "And Luna?"

Harriet looked at all the tissues discarded earlier in the waste paper basket. "I think she finally forgives me for being a mother who falls far short of her expectations."

There was something Harriet wasn't telling. Of that, Agatha was sure, but she was too tired to continue asking questions. She'd find out soon enough.

Bad news always leaks out.

The next morning, after Harriet and the children had left, Opal ordered Agatha to find her car keys.

"Grandmother, I will take you where you want to go."

"No, I must do this by myself." Opal clutched a piece of paper in her hand on which was written an address.

"Grandmother, your daughter would fire me if I let you drive off in your car. Do you want me to lose my job?"

"Then hurry up and find the keys. Time's a-wasting. I might forget what I'm about."

Once settled in the car, Opal thrust the address into Agatha's hands. "Let's go."

A North Carver address.

"Do you know how to get there, Grandmother?"

"No," she answered, as if getting there was not her problem.

From the back of the car, Agatha pulled out a Massachusetts map. She memorized the southwest route.

"Who do you know in North Carver?"

Opal signaled her to start the car. "We're wasting time."

Agatha did as she was told. It was a relatively short drive over to the town, but Agatha had to stop at the gas station to find the correct street. They pulled up in front of a small, shingled, Cape Cod house. Agatha turned off the motor. "Would you like me to come with you?"

Opal shook her head. "It's a private matter."

Agatha helped Opal out of the car, then stood back as the old woman shuffled on the footpath toward the house.

Opal knocked on the door. It swung open but Agatha could not see who it was. Opal disappeared inside.

Perhaps it's an old friend, thought Agatha. *Someone to see before she forgets who they are.*

When Opal stood at the front door of the Cape Cod house, she momentarily lost the thread. *Why am I here?*

The door opened. Standing there was a heavy-set man, unshaven, bleary-eyed, in a terry cloth bathrobe and slippers, looking as if he had been on a five-day drinking binge. "Come in," he said, backing further into the darkness.

"You look terrible," she said.

He shut the door behind her and nodded in assent.

"I'd like you to make us some tea," Opal added, thinking that would bring them into a more congenial atmosphere.

He led her into his small kitchen and filled the pot with water. "Please. Sit," he said, nodding toward his kitchen table.

Opal lowered herself down on a metal chair, while he rummaged around in a cabinet for some clean mugs and tea bags.

"Milk, sugar?" he asked.

"You look awful," she said.

He rubbed the stubble on his cheek and sighed heavily. "Outside, inside—there's no difference."

"You're feeling very sorry for yourself," opined Opal. She wished she could remember his name but, for the moment, that eluded her.

"Yes," he said.

"You love her," she said.

"Yes," he answered, his flat voice mirroring not the love but the loss.

"Well, for heaven's sake, take the bull by its horns. Go to her."

"It's not that simple. If I do that, others will get hurt. I don't have the right to bring that destruction down on her and the family."

"So you upped and left without an explanation. Where's the love in that?"

The fierceness in Opal's voice made him turn away, ashamed. He poured the hot water and handed her a cup of tea. He slumped down across from her. "This stays between us, Opal. Harriet's husband called my brother, Leon. You may remember him from Dad's trial. He's a fragile guy, volatile. About the only thing that keeps him in check is his devotion to the police force. As Speaker of the House, Mr. McWhinnie has enough influence that he can insure that my brother will lose his job if I continue to see Harriet."

"Winston wouldn't do something like that," protested Opal.

"You're wrong about that. If I kept seeing Harriet or if I even told her what her ex-husband had threatened, then Mr.

McWhinnie would make sure that the police force would suspend my brother. Based on what Leon did and didn't do with regard to the police investigation of our father, there are possible grounds for him to be fired. All it would take is a little political pressure. But if push came to shove, my brother would become a monster. He'd kill Mr. McWhinnie."

"Oh my," said Opal, "this is complicated."

"Harriet can't know why I left. Better that she thinks I don't care. But between you and me, Harriet was the best thing to ever come along in my life."

Walking to her office from the parking garage, Harriet noted that the tulips had begun to bloom. In the morning sun, the migratory birds were building nests and singing love songs to one another. Spring had finally bitten the heels of Winter. On any other day, these observations might have brought her a sense of joy and celebration, but all that she could feel was the grey mantle of despair settle upon her.

In her Boston office, Harriet stared numbly at the figures before her. She was good at what she did, managing millions of dollars of investment for wealthy bank customers. People prized her for her analytical skills, the sharpness of her questions, the ability to sift out the public relations spiel of companies to their bottom line of accounting. She didn't panic easily when the stock market shook, because she kept her eye on the long range goals of her customers. Her competency was never in question.

So why can't I concentrate? Why do I feel so leaden, weighted down into doom and gloom? Why does it matter

*whether he wants me or not? I swear, it's not worth the effort
to love a man. We were doing just fine without him.*

She knew it was a lie the minute she thought it. Harriet sat
back in her executive leather chair and openly wept.

Opal finally returned to the car where Agatha was standing
holding the door open. "I'm ready to go home now."

Agatha looked back at the house, but the front door was
already shut. She climbed into the driver's seat, started the
engine, and drove toward Duxbury.

Worry lines edged Opal's face. Her jaw moved as if trying
to chew on something. Finally, she broke the silence. "If I don't
tell someone, I'm going to forget everything. That's the way
this brain disease works."

"I'm listening, Grandmother."

"He said that Winston called."

"Who's he?"

"That man back there. What's his name? It's not important.
Winston said that he could get his brother kicked out of a job.
That he had to quit seeing her."

"Seeing who, Grandmother?"

Opal shook her head. Already, the dead-end paths of broken
synapses were fogging up her memory.

Travis picked up the phone and began dialing into the
network of judicial contacts. There were questions to be asked,
discreet inquiries. Every state had their own regulations, while
every reservation answered to the federal and tribal government.
He wanted to know exactly where Agatha Rockefeller stood
with regard to the potential charges against her.

If she was wanted for murder, it was important to find that out, to help her prepare for a defense. Running away was not a viable option. From his years served on the bench, he knew that a troubled, secret past was like a cloistered monster, devouring the flesh of the future and snacking on the bones of the present.

On the way home from North Carver, Agatha and Opal picked up Justin. Agatha fed them both lunch, then Opal settled into her rocking chair for her afternoon nap, while Justin read his library books. Everywhere Agatha went, Digger dogged her steps, not wanting ever again to be left to his own instincts. He had changed from a wild Sheltie into a timid lapdog.

Sola's room looked like a whirlwind had passed, that swirled not leaves but books, clothes, shoes, and scraps of paper all over the floor. Agatha folded the clean clothes into a pile and threw the dirty ones into a hamper. She stacked Sola's books on the end table, then set about raking up the pieces of paper with her fingers. In large, scrawling penmanship, Sola had written a scatter of thoughts:

I am a boy girl. Or a girl boy? I had a penis once at my belly button, but they cut it off. Too many operations.

There are dead people around us all the time. They stand there in the background, next to real people. Luna tells me they're not there, that I'm crazy.

The ground shivers. Nobody else feels it. I'm scared I'll fall off. Mommy says that the earth will hold me, but I don't believe it.

Mommy and Justin are nice. Miz Stands is nice. Her boyfriend is nice. Tom is nice. Luna is not.

Daddy calls me Princess.

Something's missing in me. Deep down missing. God left it out.

They called me Spazz, because of my cerebral palsy. It hurts. A lot. But I still believe in the goodness of people everywhere. Even Luna.

When Sola arrived home that afternoon, she didn't even notice that her bedroom had been cleaned. She dumped her books on the floor and dropped her jacket on the bed.

Luna appeared a half hour later and headed to the kitchen for a snack. She slathered a measured tablespoon of peanut butter on a piece of rye cracker and poured herself an eight ounce glass of skim milk, then noted the calorie count in a food diary. She had kept her promise not to binge eat and purge, finding a substitute satisfaction in the control of caloric intake. Agatha insisted that she take in a minimum of eighteen hundred calories a day, so as not to exchange bulimia for anorexia.

"I'm being good as gold," she said to Agatha who was in the living room setting up a jigsaw puzzle for Justin.

"Who lives in North Carver?" asked Agatha.

Luna shrugged her shoulders. "Why do you want to know?"

"I drove your grandmother over there this morning. She was quite disturbed by a conversation she had with a man there. It has to do with your father making threats."

Luna stopped chewing her cracker for a second. She put down her glass of milk and picked up a Rolodex. "Here's the family telephone book with addresses." She thumbed through the A's and some of the B's, before saying, "Look."

Her finger rested on a North Carver address for Tom Breslin. "What did Dad say to him?"

"Your grandmother wasn't too clear about it. I gather that your Dad threatened to get his brother fired from the police force. What does that have to do with your Mom?"

"Tom broke off with Mom last night with no explanation. This is all Dad's doing. Son of a bitch," Luna exclaimed. "Why can't he leave Mom alone? She deserves to have a life too."

For Agatha, it was all beginning to fall into place: Harriet's depression, her remark of their having exhausted their welcome with Tom, Opal's determination to set things right.

Luna headed straight to the telephone and dialed a number.

Sola called out from the bathroom, "Could somebody get me some toilet paper?"

As she headed toward the stairs, Agatha wondered if Luna was calling Tom Breslin to read him the riot act.

If Opal couldn't change his mind, then nobody can.

The telephone rang five times before Tom answered it. Frankly, he had no taste for conversation with his brother, his colleagues, or telemarketers. In a gruff voice, he barked, "Yes?"

"Tom?" A tentative voice spoke. It was Harriet.

His heart sank. Immediately he knew who it was tethered on the other end of the line. "I'm so sorry."

"At first, I thought it was a matter of dignity, that I shouldn't pursue you, that I should simply let go. Then I thought I would surely lose you. You'd wander off into some back alley of my life and memory. You'd become the man I had once dated, once loved. Then, years down the line, I wouldn't remember you so well, how you looked, how you smell, the sound of your voice, the touch of your hands." She began crying. "I couldn't bear that."

"Harriet, I love you."

"Then come home to me," she begged.

A car drove up Cranberry Lane. "Tell Mom I'll be home late." Before Agatha could question her, Luna grabbed her jacket, ran out of the house, and jumped into the car.

As if waking up from a self-induced coma, Digger leapt up and attacked the door, scratching to get outside and herd Luna back inside.

"Our old Digger has finally returned," announced Agatha.

"He's crazy," said Justin.

"No he's not," said Sola, leaning over and petting Digger's head. "Are you, boy?"

Digger thumped his tail on the floor.

"When is Mom getting home?" asked Justin.

"I'm hungry. When is dinner?" asked Sola.

"When will Edgar get here?" asked Opal.

Agatha rolled her eyes before heading to the kitchen.

Panting, Digger sniffed the air for the scent of food, then flopped down by the door to await Luna's return.

"I'll stay down here and wait for you," said Caitlin. "Here are the papers you need."

Luna exited the car and rang her father's apartment bell. The buzzer indicated he was there. The building's front door opened and let her through. When she arrived at his floor, she knocked on the door.

"Yes?" her father answered, as he opened the door. "What a wonderful surprise. What are you doing here, Princess?"

Luna marched past him into the apartment. "I won't stay long, Father."

"You're sounding rather formal. What's the problem?"

Luna sat down on the living room couch. "You and Mom are divorced from each other."

"Yes, you know that." He sat down opposite her.

"So you each have the right to date whomever you want?"

"Of course. What's the point?"

"Why are you meddling in Mom's life?"

"What do you mean? She's free to date."

"Then why did you threaten Tom?"

"Tom? Who's Tom?" Winston sat back in his chair, folding his hands on his lap.

Luna couldn't believe that her Dad was trying to play dumb, the same way she used to respond to her mother when questioned about smoking.

Winston could sense the incredulity of his daughter, her impatience with him. "You mean the guy with the killer father?" he added.

"You warned him that his brother would get fired if Tom continued to see Mom."

"I didn't call Tom. I don't need to make threats." That was, at least, a partial truth. Winston had telephoned Leon, not Tom, knowing that Leon would pass along the message.

For an exasperated moment, Luna was tempted to call her father "a slime ball" and rush out of the apartment in anger. *But that wouldn't solve anything. It would only let him win the argument. Have patience. Think*, she cautioned herself.

From her knapsack, she pulled out the copied bank statements, the trail of illegal payments by the drug companies, and the names of the donors. She handed them to her father, then stood up to leave.

His mouth dropped open as he perused them.

"Where did you get these?" he asked, his brow stern and furious.

"There are other copies. Unless you stop harassing Mom, they may become public." Then remembering Caitlin's instructions, she added, "The Family Act needs to be amended so that the drug companies don't profit. And, of course, you need to return their money because, otherwise, you'll always be vulnerable."

"Are you threatening me, Luna? Your own father?" Swelling up with anger, he rose from his chair.

Shaking with fear and trying to hide it, Luna answered, "No, Dad. I don't need to make threats. I trust that, as my father, you will do the right thing." She looked him straight in the eye.

It was a staring contest.

She was young and untested. He was the old bull, cornered, a red flag flapping in his face.

And then he blinked.

TWENTY-FIVE

Harriet called home to say she'd be late and to eat without her. The others waited for Luna. Upon her arrival, she pulled Agatha aside and proudly described the confrontation with her father. Together, they set the table and called the family to sit down.

"Have I now earned the right to call you Agatha?" asked Luna.

Agatha nodded. "My shortened name is 'Stands,' but my full ceremonial names is 'Stands Her Ground.' It means that when I know what is right, I do it. Just as you did with your father."

"I'd like to discover my real name, Agatha Stands Her Ground," twitted Luna.

"If you'd like, I'll take you to a Native American ceremony where you can do just that."

"A name like yours?"

Opal looked up from her book. "Luna's real name is 'She Talks A Lot.'"

"Can I get a name too?" asked Justin.

"Someday." answered Agatha. "One needs a name to grow into. Sometimes, I've stood my ground. Sometimes, I've cut and run. But my name reminds me what I should do. It's a name the Spirits gave me."

"King of the World," announced Justin. "That'll be my name."

"What about you, Sola?" asked Opal. "What do you think your ceremonial name should be?"

Sola shrugged her shoulders, sighed, and gave great thought to the matter. She then whispered the name into Opal's ear, before heading off to the bathroom to wash her hands.

"Well?" pestered Luna. "What name did she pick?"

"Princess," Opal answered.

Travis arrived as Agatha was serving the dessert: a cranberry-apple compote topped with vanilla ice cream. "Just in time, I see," he said, rubbing his belly and pulling up a chair.

He sampled the dessert. "A fine cook you are, Agatha Stands."

"Agatha Stands Her Ground," trumpeted Justin.

"She certainly does that," Travis said, winking at her. "I'm hoping to take her back to her old stomping grounds this summer. I think they have a sun dance out there."

Agatha's eyebrows squinched together. She shook her head. "No, I can't go back there. Ever."

"Oh, but you can," he said.

"Don't you want to return to your old home?" asked Sola.

"My husband is buried there," Agatha answered, darting piercing looks at Travis who, at that moment, had his mouth full of fruit and ice cream.

"It would make you too sad?" asked Sola.

"I didn't know you had been married," complained Luna.

Travis cheerfully ignored Agatha's warning glances. "Her husband was cremated and buried there. Her people know she left because she was in grief. They want her to come back and visit."

"You've been snooping," said Agatha.

"Guilty as charged," he answered, digging into a second helping of compote. "Really, you're a marvelous cook."

"Would you come back to us?" asked Sola.

"Of course." Agatha frowned, then queried Travis. "You mean I could go there free and clear?"

Travis nodded. "Jesse's mother said she thought that you had lost the directions and didn't know how to get back home. I told her that I had a good map and would bring you back for a visit. That made her very happy."

Much to the astonishment of all the children, but not to Opal, Agatha scooted around the table and planted a kiss upon Travis' fruited lips.

"Will you marry me?" Tom asked. They were parked in the driveway of Two Cranberry Lane. It was dark outside, but the house glowed with brilliant light.

"Of course, I will," answered Harriet, "If you'll have all of us."

"It's a big house," he said. "I think it has room for one more lost soul."

"Let's tell them," said Harriet.

"Now?"

"Yes, now."

Arm in arm, they headed toward the front door. Digger greeted their arrival with excited barks and dancing feet. Tom pushed open the door.

The family had gathered around the table, finishing up the dessert. They pushed their chairs together to make room for them.

"Have you eaten?" asked Agatha.

"Yes," said Harriet. "Everyone, we have an announcement to make."

Clasping Tom's hand, she looked affectionately around the table at each individual: Justin with ice cream dribbling down his chin, Sola's headphones dangling around her neck, Luna beaming with new confidence, Opal grinning and patting her hair in place, Agatha with her hand on Travis' shoulder, and Digger sniffing around the floor for fallen crumbs. This was her family. This was her life.

"We're going to be married," said Harriet.

"Does that mean we have to move?" asked Justin, his forehead wrinkled with concern.

"Tom will join us here." Harriet smiled.

"It would be a privilege for me to become part of this family," added Tom.

"Wow, that's cool," said Luna, covertly slipping Digger crumbs from her plate.

"Congratulations," echoed Agatha and Travis, grinning at each other.

"Yes!" cheered Opal, winking at Tom. "Edgar has finally come home."

"No more divorces, Mom," pleaded Sola, her face shifting from happy to anxious.

"That's right, darling. No more dropping of the ball. This time it's forever."

Around the messy table at Two Cranberry Lane, each voice a thread, separate in tone and texture, in age and experience, in desire and destiny, but woven into the family tapestry, each voice a part of a whole choral recitation: "Forever is a very long time."

"Grandma," asked Sola, needing the comfort of old rituals in the face of new changes, "Could you tell us that story again?"

"Which story is that, dear one?"

"The one about the labyrinth," answered Sola.

"And the monster," said Justin.

"And the handsome hero," added Luna.

"And the woman," said Harriet.

"And the magic ball of thread," concluded Agatha.

The End

RESOURCES

VCFS Syndrome/Deletion 22q11.2

Velo-Cardio-Facial Syndrome Educational Foundation, Inc.
  at http://www.vcfsef.org or
  PO Box 874, Milltown, New Jersey 08850
  Telephone: (214) 360-4740 or 1-866-VCF-SEF5.

International 22q11.2 Deletion Syndrome Foundation, Inc.
  at http://www.22q.org
  22 Tanforan Court,Matawan, NJ 07747
  1-877-739-1849

Alzheimer's Disease

Alzheimer's Association
  at http://www.alz.org or
  225 N. Michigan Ave, Suite 1700, Chicago, IL 60601
  1-800-272-3900

ADEAR—Alzheimer's Disease Education & Referral Center
  at http://www.alzheimers.nia.nih.gov
  National Institute on Aging, Bldg. 31, Rm 5C27,
  31 Center Drive, MSC 2292, Bethesda, MD 20892
  1-800-438-4380

Eating Disorders

NEDA—National Eating Disorders Association
  at http://www.nationaleatingdisorders.org
  603 Stewart St, Suite 803, Seattle, WA 98101
  1-800-931-2237

REFERENCES

Quote:

1. Shakespeare, William. 1597. *All's Well That Ends Well* (Act IV, sc.3, lines 83-84) from *The Complete Plays and Poems of William Shakespeare*. Boston: Houghton Mifflin Co., 1942, p. 380

Chapter One:

1. Shakespeare, William. 1600. *As You Like It* (Act II, sc.7, lines 139-141) from *The Complete Plays and Poems of William Shakespeare*. Boston: Houghton Mifflin Co., 1942, p. 225

Chapter Six:

1. Frost, Robert. 1923. "Stopping By Woods On A Snowy Evening." from *The Poetry of Robert Frost*, Ed. Edward Connery Lathem. New York: Holt, Rhinehart & Winston, 1969, pp 224-5